Ohio Ghost Hunt

By Jannette Qu

Check out other Ohio G

Haunted Hocking—Ghost Hunter's Guide to the Hocking
(Covers the Hocking Hills Region)

Haunted Hocking— A Ghost Hunter's Guide II
(Hocking Hills and the counties of Athens, Lawrence, Meigs, Fairfield, Perry, Ross, Vinton, and Scioto)

Ohio Ghost Hunter's Guide — Haunted Hocking III
(Covers Counties of: Allen, Athens, Delaware, Franklin, Gallia, Hancock, Henry, Highland, Hocking, Jackson, Lake, Licking, Lorain, Lucas, Marion, Muskingum, Perry, Pike, Sandusky, Scioto, Washington and Wood)

Ohio Ghost Hunter Guide—Franklin County IV
(Covers Columbus and Vicinity)

Ohio Ghost Hunter Guide —Haunted Hocking V
(Covers Allen, Auglaize, Butler, Champaign, Clark, Clinton, Crawford, Cuyahoga, Delaware, Franklin, Gallia, Greene, Hardin, Highland, Hocking, Jackson, Jefferson, Knox, Lake, Lawrence, Logan, Lucas, Madison, Miami, Mahoning, Montgomery, Morgan, Muskingum, Pickaway, Pike, Putnam, Richland, Ross, Sandusky, Scioto, Stark, Summit, Vinton, Warren, Wood)

Ohio Ghost Hunter Guide —Haunted Hocking VI
(Covers Adams, Ashtabula, Belmont, Brown, Clark, Clermont, Coshocton, Cuyahoga, Defiance, Delaware, Erie, Fairfield, Fayette, Fulton, Greene, Guernsey, Hamilton, Hancock, Henry, Hocking, Jackson, Knox, Marion, Medina, Morrow, Pickaway, Pike, Sandusky, Scioto, Summit, Tuscarawas, Vinton, Warren, Wayne)

Cleveland Ohio Ghost Hunter Guide —Haunted Hocking VII
(Haunted Cleveland, Cuyahoga County and Vicinity)

Ohio Ghost Hunter Guide—Haunted Hocking VIII
(Covers Adams, Ashland, Athens, Brown, Butler, Champaign, Columbiana, Cuyahoga, Fairfield, Hocking, Jackson, Jefferson, Knox, Licking, Lorain, Lucas, Madison, Mahoning, Marion, Medina, Ottawa, Perry, Pickaway, Preble, Ross, Sandusky, Scioto, Summit, Trumbull, Vinton, Washington, Wyandot)

ISBN-10:
1940087112

ISBN-13:
978-1-940087-11-5

21 Crows Dusk to Dawn
Publishing, 21 Crows, LLC

DEDICATION—
For Mom and Aunt Mary who like the ghosties too.

Cover image top: Ivan Bliznetsov
Cover image back top: Eric Vega

Disclaimer: The stories and legends in this book are for enjoyment purposes and taken from many different resources. Many have been passed down and have been altered along the way. The authors attempt to sort through the many different variations found on a story and find the most popular and the most supported by historical evidence. Not all sources and legends can be substantiated. We try to give you the basic research and history so you can delve into the stories, enjoy them, discover something new.

Potential Ghost Hunters should always respect the areas to search out the paranormal and also respect those who are still living who might be related to the dead. Public properties may become private after the printing of the book or they may simply be listed with the address so you know the historical area where the story originated. Regardless if the area is listed as private or not, please respect the landowner and do not disturb their privacy. Listing the GPS and address does not imply you are welcome to visit, nor that you visit without contacting the property owner. It is to give you a visual of the location where the haunting occurred. Call ahead of time to make sure you are not trespassing.

Ghost hunting can be a dangerous endeavor due to the many different environmental factors including many that are done in the darkness, forests, in old buildings or in hazardous areas. Before visiting any haunted site, verify location, accessibility and safety. We never recommend venturing into unknown areas in darkness or entering private or public property without prior permission. GPS routes may change or become hazardous. Always check with owners/operators of public and private areas to see if a license is needed to hunt and to check for unsafe areas. Make sure you follow all laws and abide by the rules of any private or public region you use. Readers assume full responsibility for use of information in this book.

The background images were taken at the actual site of the haunted area, if applicable and available. Other images were added to illustrate what others have seen. For those who would like to share their ghost story occurring in Ohio or surrounding states, contact us through hauntedhocking.com. We would love to hear from you!

Table of Contents—Ghost Hunter Guide

Table of Contents—Ghost Hunter Guide

Table of Contents—Ghost Hunter Guide

Table of Contents—Ghost Hunter Guide

Table of Contents—Ghost Hunter Guide

Yawning Grave

It was Tuesday, December 19th of 1893 when the sleepy village of Winchester, just about 15 miles from the town seat of West Union, awakened to the horrible news of the murders of 80 year-old Luther "Pitt" Rhine and his 71 year-old wife, Martha. The elderly couple had been eking out a modest living on a small farm tucked along the stream of Elk Fork. Both had been found with their skulls crushed and their throats slashed from ear to ear. It appeared Luther Rhine had been soundly sleeping when first attacked. After being beaten on the head, he had slipped from the bed where his throat was viciously cut. His body was found upon the floor. Martha Rhine fought for her life; the room showed signs of struggle. Her head was nearly severed from her body.

Fingers in the surrounding towns quickly pointed to a sixteen year-old boy, Roscoe Parker, whose family consisting of a mother and three children, helped with odd jobs at the Rhine's farm. Around town, they were thought of as an ornery lot of bad character and the mother was described as "notoriously tough."

On Saturday December 16th, Roscoe had helped Luther drive a calf to nearby Winchester for butchering.

The gently rolling hills and charming backdrop of farms in Adams County near Winchester and North Liberty hardly seem a setting for an unspeakable murder and a ghost.

The boy watched carefully as Luther was paid $13.00 for the calf. He chatted heartily with the man about the large sum during the entire ride home. The next day, Sunday the 17th, would be the last time any of the neighbors saw the couple alive. Two days later, Luther and Martha were found dead, bludgeoned to death in their bedclothes on the bedroom floor. The money Luther had collected for the calf was gone.

. . .The story of the discovery and condition of the victims is revolting in the extreme. It seems that the old man was first struck while asleep on the bed, whence he rolled to the floor, where his throat was cut. The old lady seems to have fought desperately for her life, as the room showed evidences of the struggle, and her hands were badly, cut where she had grasped the fatal butcher knife. She was found with her head nearly severed from her body. The house cat which had been shut up with them had eaten their noses and ears. Great excitement prevails over this terrible butchery. **The News-Herald. (Hillsboro, Ohio) December 28, 1893, Page 5. An Awful Double Crime.**

It was no surprise to those who knew the Parkers that five dollars of the Rhine's money identified as being paid for the calf was found hidden in a bed at Roscoe Parker's home. A pair of Luther's stockings was also found and Roscoe's clothing was covered in blood. Neighbors of the Rhines saw Roscoe leaving the scene of the crime just after the murder. Two sticks with matted hair and blood were collected and angry neighbors of the Rhines decided to take the law into their own hands and hang the boy for his alleged crime.

Roscoe Parker was whisked off to the West Union Jail. Then, for his own safety he was taken to the Scioto County Jail in Portsmouth. However, his luck would run out when he was returned to the West Union Jail for trial. A mob broke into the jail, overtaking the sheriff, Marion Dunlap, and his deputy. They broke down the doors to the jail, walked Roscoe ten miles in his underclothes to a spot between Winchester and North Liberty. Then the frenzied mob hung the boy from a tree, riddled his body with bullets.

CINCINNATI, Jan. 12. Roscoe Parker, the colored boy who four weeks ago last Sunday night brutally murdered aged Mr. Rhine and his wife, was hanged by a mob of the best citizens of Winchester and adjacent points, In Adams County, O., at 1 o'clock this morning, about four miles from Winchester.
The murder was for money, and only $10 was obtained. Parker, the murderer, was only sixteen years old and has worked for the old couple and had known of Mr. Rhine receiving money for sale of some stock. The boy confessed his crime, but implicated Sam Johnson, who easily proved his innocence. **The Evening World. (New York) January 12, 1894. BROOKLYN LAST EDITION. Hanged by "Best Citizens"**

But Roscoe Parker's story doesn't end there. In fact, as far as ghosts go, it was just the very beginning.

Pauper's Corner of Cherry Fork Cemetery (rear of graves).

His body was eventually buried in the northwest corner (then known as the 'pauper's corner') of North Liberty's Cherry Fork Cemetery by an ex-slave known as Sam Bradley. Not long after, someone found that Roscoe's grave had been dug up. Upon further inspection, it was discovered that the dead young man's coffin had been opened and his head was missing, cut completely from his body. Its whereabouts remained a mystery.

A couple years later on a hot Wednesday night, August 6th of 1896, Maurice Hudson, a local farmer, noticed a strange sound when he passed Cherry Fork Cemetery. As he peered cautiously into the graveyard, his eyes opened wide with shock. Over one grave, a ghostly man stood with arms outstretched and his hands opened wide.

> . . . The body was headless, that is, so far as the head being connected with the body is concerned. Hudson states that from the neck there spurted upward a conical stream of blood to the hight (height) of five or six feet, where it was probably two feet in circumference. Dancing on the top of this stream of blood and bouncing about in every conceivable position was the head of the apparition.
>
> After spending its force on the head the blood descended over and around the form in a spray. Down the palms of the outstretched hands of the figure there seemed to spurt a thousand small streams, so that the apparition presented the appearance of a small garden fountain. Hudson claims he was rooted to the spot for fully five minutes, and that when he did finally make a step the wonderful picture began to gradually fade from view, and the soft pale light which had surrounded the scene for a radius of probably fifty feet grew dimmer and dimmer. In the meantime, the head had begun to glow with a bright light and by the time the body had faded from view it had become brilliantly illuminated, and together with a trail of fire ten feet in length took its flight in a westerly direction, resembling a comet, and after a distance of probably 500 yards fell to the ground. . . **Cleveland Plain Dealer. (Cleveland, Ohio) Historical Archives. August 12, 1896. A Grave Yawns.**

Mister Hudson stood paralyzed as the scene unfolded before his eyes. An investigation of the location the next morning exposed the truth. The grave where the headless apparition appeared with blood streaming from its neck belonged to Roscoe Parker. Throughout the years thereafter, people claimed to see balls of light flitting from grave to grave at Cherry Fork Cemetery. They would hear strange noises from the unmarked grave of the murdered young man who was said to have murdered two others.

Katotawa Creek
530 US-42
Ashland, Ohio 44805
40.898148, -82.229826

The Ghost of Katotawa

Around 1762, Mohicans established a village on a hill about a half mile from the town of Jeromesville called Mohican Johnstown. Although it was surrounded by marsh and swamp, the tribe lived there contentedly hunting and raising corn along the bottomland until they were forcibly removed during the War of 1812.

The banks of Katotawa Creek and the gravesite of the Mohican who haunts the creek and land.

Many of these Native Indians joined the British forces against the United States. Some even tried to stay behind on their land. Among the Mohicans who remained was a friendly, elderly chief by the name of Katotawa who set up a hut along the banks of a small creek where he once loved to fish and hunt. There, he lived alone for many years undisturbed until he was found dead, beheaded by an unknown attacker.

He was buried on a hill near what is now Township Road 553. However, his spirit has never come to rest. A headless Katotawa has been seen on dark and foggy nights along the banks of the creek that now bears his name—Katotawa Creek. He is carrying his head and blood pours down his shoulders and arms.

Landoll's Mohican Castle

Landoll's Mohican Castle

The Landoll's Mohican Castle was built in 1996 by Jim Landoll, much of it with timber felled from a tornado along with field stones left behind by early settlers farming the land. It is a sight to see coming up through the wild hills that have snuck out of Mohican Memorial State Forest and now surround the grounds.

It is turrets and towers and beautiful sandstone walls with luxurious guest suites and charming cottages and . . . perhaps a few ghosts. You may wonder how something so new and not-so-scary-looking could actually cough up a ghost or two. The castle, itself, is a more modern mirror of the castles of old. It certainly isn't bleak or forbidding. But it isn't the castle that seems to hold the spirits, although the spirit of a Civil War soldier has been seen once in a while in the rooms. It is the land and the inhabitants of old that come back to visit the living every once in a while.

You see, there was once a church tucked into the property along with its cemetery. According to Jim Landoll, it was built atop the hill by Jacob Heyd in the 1830s, shared by the community and named Saint Jacobs Lutheran Church. There were both German-speaking and English-speaking parishioners, and it was believed that around the 1840s there was a dispute over which language would be used in the church. It was determined that English would become the customary language, and resentful, the Germans dug up their family members buried in the cemetery and reinterred them in a new cemetery down the road. Strangely, not long after the rift between the two oppositions the church suspiciously burned to the ground. Mysteriously, the record book for the church had several pages missing. They were ripped away and never found.

The Saint Jacobs Lutheran Church Cemetery at the castle. A ghostly girl in a blue dress has been seen wandering the graves.

Cursed, the land might be. At least that is what some believe. Since purchasing the property, the Landolls have also been plagued by fires – the family's publishing company burned to the ground and when it was moved, more fires occurred at the new building. To make matters worse, a million dollar restaurant on the property burned down in 2008.

A little girl in a blue dress has been seen inside the cemetery.

But ghosts . . . yes, people have seen a few spirits here too. A tiny graveyard still stands at the peak of a hill, well-maintained and nestled quietly beneath the pines. Not far away, once stood the church that burned to the ground. Jim Landoll affirms crying has been heard coming from somewhere in the cemetery and a little girl in a blue dress roaming the graves has been reported to staff.

Haunted Cottage 13.

And then there is the cute, little stone cottage. Just off the gravel lane leading to the castle, it is home to the ghost of a former owner. Voices and footsteps have been heard inside the building. Even the apparition of the previous owner, himself, has been seen by paranormal research groups renting the cottage. And by the way, you might be able to see a ghost too. Jim Landoll welcomes ghost hunters to rent the cottage and vie for an unforgettable, spirited experience on this unique property.

Haunted Tunnel

The tunnel has many ghost stories.

There are almost as many legends associated with the Haunted Tunnel outside Ashland as there are generations who have visited it. So how do you find the truth behind the folklore, choose the story that really existed? Sometimes you simply can't. However, here are a few popular ones passed from word of mouth—

So the story goes like this: Once upon a time, in a small Ohio farming community outside Ashland, children began to disappear at an alarming rate.

Folks knew who it was that was snatching up their children, a witch who used them in her ritual sacrifices. Outraged, the farmers hunted her down and hung her in a bridge tunnel. Now, if you drive through the tunnel, stop, turn off your lights and put your car in neutral, ghostly hands will push your car to the opposite end. (Of course, we don't recommend this stunt. It is a road that still has traffic.)

The Haunted Tunnel.

Or the story could go like this: Once upon a time, there was a house near the bridge. In the house lived a loving couple who were preparing for the birth of their first child. However, the woman and baby died. In his horrendous grief, the man hung himself from the tunnel. Now, if you drive to the tunnel and honk three times, you can see the man hanging there.

Phantom Horseman of Dead Man's Hill

Cherry Hill in Fayette County had a headless horseman that stalked residents along the roadways, drives, and fields off State Route 38 near Yatesville. Stumpy's Hollow in Muskingum County had a headless man appear in a ravine at night that frightened those walking the roadway in the 19th century. But who would have known that Athens County was once known for a place called "Dead Man's Hill" that was haunted by its own phantom horseman?

> *In the southern part of Athens county, Ohio, an extensive elevation, denominated "Dead Man's Hill," is haunted by a phantom horseman. The clattering of equine hoofs may be heard nightly and the wail of an unfortunate being in agony is sometimes described to be heartrending. This apparition with a dead rider on its back sometimes dashes furiously toward travelers, through whom it passes like a misty cloud, leaving them clammy and almost dead with chill and terror. The noise of the approaching phantom steed is said to resemble the rushing sound produced by an eagle in its most rapid flight.*
> ***Philadelphia Inquirer (Philadelphia, PA) October 14, 1889: Spooks and Spirits***

Ghost Hollow—Followed By Ghostly Hounds

The roads east of Ripley that two men took one cold night in February were ones they had taken many times before. Folks had talked about ghosts along their path. The men did not believe the stories until something incredibly terrifying occurred to them . . .

It wasn't the first time the ghostly hounds were heard. Nor would it be the last. Those along the rugged wooded hills and hidden, dark hollows tucked within the embrace of Eagle Creek and along the remote roads and old footpaths like Eagle Creek, North Pole and Martin Hill near Ripley had been whispering about the peculiar sights and eerie sounds for quite some time. In fact, many called the hollow nearby: *Ghost Hollow.* It seemed farfetched, what they said, almost preposterous. But on a cold night in February, two Brown County men got a taste of that unbelievable. . .

Thirty-six year-old Alexander Griffith and 59 year-old Ephraim "Tip" Martin were returning from a trip to Ripley. The two had been visiting friends. Both were farmers and well known in the area. They were respected men, trusted pillars in the community. They were the kind of men whose word was good and true with nothing more than a handshake. Their families came from decent, pioneer stock and Alexander Griffith had been a Brown county commissioner. But something would happen on the chilly Thursday, January 31st of 1895, that would cause more than a few to question the two men's credibility. And perhaps they even questioned themselves on what they would see that night coming home from town. In fact, their foes in nearby Hillsboro would throw it back into their faces, trying to smear their reputation when their secret was revealed—

The Adams county liar is out in the Cleveland Press with a ghost story. The scene is laid in a ravine near Ripley. Ex County Commissioner Griffith, of Brown county is accredited with having seen a groaning apparition dragging a log chain over the wild hillside. . . The News-Herald. (Hillsboro, Ohio) February 21, 1895

The old roads like Eagle Creek and Martin Hill that the men would have travelled are surrounded by ravines and valleys thick with trees and brush. . .and dark at night.

But both men saw the apparition. And they were sure enough of their judgement to tell the story to the local newspapers. So what exactly happened to cause such a fervent stir in the community and force two good men to question their judgement and, perhaps, their rationality? Their story went like this:

It was cold out that Thursday night. Alexander Griffith and his friend and neighbor, Tip Martin, were working their way along a brutally chilly trek six miles back from the town of Ripley along the Ohio River. The land dips and flows in the county, rugged steep hills with thick trees meet with fertile farm fields. Within, dark pockets of hollows flow in and out along the Beetle Creek and Eagle Creek. It wasn't a pleasant journey in February and woolen hats were firmly placed on the heads and coats warmly tucked around bodies. A scarf around the neck could be pulled up to cover the nose and lips and stop the frigid air from leaving the red insult of chapped windburned cheeks to suffer the next day.

Griffith and Martin were just about to enter a ravine that night when something strangely akin to an agonizing groan caught their attention. At first they thought someone was injured so they paused in their route and looked around. Finding no source to the sound, they assumed it was the wind working its way through the trees and so the two farmers continued onward.

But the men would only take a few steps when to the right of where they stood and along a steep hill, the figure of a man dragging a heavy chain came running down the slope. They watched in utter shock until it disappeared. Then, as they resumed a much quicker pace and came out to open space again, the sound of baying dogs filled the air. Suddenly, a pack of foxhounds appeared from the darkness as if following the strange form dragging the chain. Then, they too disappeared completely from view.

The men continued home, digesting the macabre scene that had played out before them. It was enough to make a man question his sanity. But there was a story behind the strange apparition that may have added credence to what they saw. . .

In 1878, a fox drive was advertised, and a circuit of five miles was made. At 1 o'clock in the afternoon the army was centering, and in the circuit were ten or fifteen foxes. "Joe" Woods, a surly revengeful character, came up with ten large hounds. The dogs made several attempts to break the ring. Seeing the dogs fail Joe kicked up a battle with the captain, and a fight followed. When the lines broke the dogs rushed through and gave chase to the foxes, breaking the circle, and neither foxes nor dogs were ever seen again. Losing the foxes made the hunters so angry that they took Woods to a large stump, secured a big log chain and fastened him. He was then left to get away as best he could. That night Woods escaped and was never seen again. **Cleveland Plain Dealer. (Cleveland, Oh) February 9, 1895. Followed By Ghostly Hounds**

A fox hunt centered in the ravine. A tough character by the name of Joe Woods brought in ten of his hounds and demanded that his dogs be added to the hunt. During this time, a fight arose. In the confusion, the foxes escaped. Infuriated, the hunters grabbed up Joe Woods, tied him to a stump with chains and left him to die. The men were sure the ghost they saw was Woods. No one ever saw Woods or his dogs again.

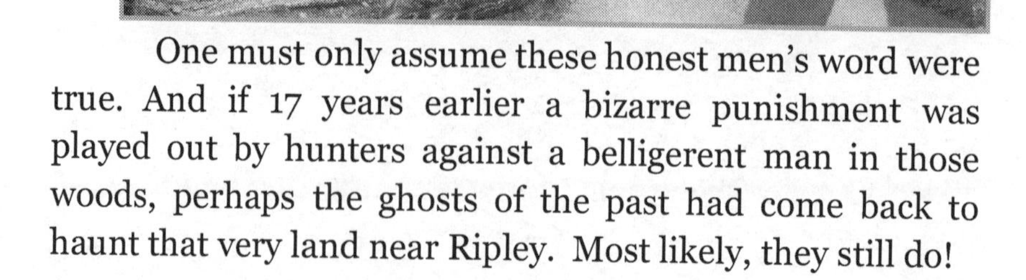

One must only assume these honest men's word were true. And if 17 years earlier a bizarre punishment was played out by hunters against a belligerent man in those woods, perhaps the ghosts of the past had come back to haunt that very land near Ripley. Most likely, they still do!

In 1826, settlers had just begun to eke out an existence in the small village of Collinsville, Ohio. Like many communities of its time, there was a sprinkling of businesses centered around farming– saw and grist mills, a blacksmith and wagon maker shop, homes, a school and Presbyterian Church. Small cabins dotted the landscape and the outlying area was still much-covered in thick woodland. It wasn't long before men came to the area to help clear the land for farming.

Two such men by the name of Wells and Clarkson, hailing from Missouri, attained work cutting trees between the towns of Darrtown and Collinsville in Milford Township. They built a small cabin along the rugged trail between the two towns (Darrtown is about four miles from Collinsville) and made friends with their closest neighbors. One man in particular came to know the Missourians quite well, a Mister Williston who lived less than a mile away. In fact, he was quite surprised when calling upon the two one cool November day to find them gone and the cabin completely deserted. Wells and Clarkson had simply disappeared.

Two months would pass. After struggling to find out the men's whereabouts, their friends in Collinsville all but gave up ever seeing the two missing woodcutters again. Then one day, Williston was passing by an older section of a local cemetery and he noted that, strangely, there was a fresher burial with leaves carefully placed on top as if to camouflage the newer condition of the grave. Curious, Williston got the help of a neighbor. The two reluctantly dug into the fresh dirt only to find the scant and decaying remains of Clarkson—his head had been completely severed from his body and the head was nowhere to be found. The Cincinnati Enquirer would write the following in 1890:

> . . . Some two months after this, as Williston was passing near this old graveyard, his attention was called to a newly made grave, which was partially covered with leaves. Williston, in company with a man named Kingston, opened the grave, and to their astonishment they found the decayed remains of Clarkson, the head being severed from the body and not found. The body was replaced in the lonely grave as they knew little of the past history of the two men, Wells and Clarkson. All efforts to find Wells proved of no avail, but it has since been ascertained that he died in an Alms House in Berks County, Pennsylvania and on his death-bed he confessed to the murder of Clarkson. ***Cincinnati Enquirer (Cincinnati, Ohio) September 14, 1890.***

It wasn't long after Williston found the body that a headless man wrapped in a sheet and perched on the stump of a large, cut Sycamore tree would appear to those passing the cemetery. Being along a main route between Darrtown and Collinsville, many carriage riders would tell their harrowing tales of seeing the headless apparition. Some believed. Some did not.

Almost nightly now and then can be seen what appears to be a headless man wrapped in a sheet, perched upon the stump of a large sycamore tree with blood streaming down his body, and in a short space of time vanishes from sight. For some time past, at night, when the moon is in its splendor, has this spectacle been viewed by many of the inhabitants of that vicinity. Since it has become public there is a vast amount of excitement throughout that portion of Butler County, and it is the firm belief that it is the ghost of the murdered man Clarkson. For many years past there has been a path leading from Collinsville through this section, and one through the adjoining fields on the north that made a short route from Collinsville to Darrtown and many an inhabitant of these two villages has traced this path at almost all hours of the night, but since the discovery of this strange apparition, they manage to get to their homes before nightfall, or take the public road for fear of seeing this strange object in the woods.
Cincinnati Enquirer. (Cincinnati, Ohio) September 14, 1890.

The Collinsville Cemetery and the area where the headless ghost of Clarkson is said to appear.

However, there wasn't a soul in the two towns who would deny the headless ghost was the murdered Clarkson. Many would try to hunt the ghost down, sure it was nothing more than a hoax. But no one ever caught it. So if you are driving along a certain section of roadway between Darrtown and Collinsville near the Collinsville Cemetery, take a quick peek toward the older section of graves at the cemetery and skim across the outlying area where the trees are old and large. You may, too, see the ghost perched on an old Sycamore stump with blood streaming down his body.

The Collinsville Cemetery—note the foggy patch and the ball of light in the bottom right corner of the image.

The newspaper noted that the property and graveyard where the ghost was seen was on a wooded section of land between the area where the McMechan and Keil farms would later be located during the 1890s. The graveyard where Clarkson's body was found, it was reported, was ancient even in 1826 when the murder occurred. It may have been across the road from where the Collinsville Presbyterian Church once stood and the Collinsville Cemetery now stands. On the 1836 plat map, there is a Meeting House marked which was across the street from where the cemetery is now. There could have been burials here with early pioneers like the Richards and the Simpsons that are long forgotten. Known graves at the Collinsville Cemetery only date back to the 1830s , but it is the only cemetery listed in the 1836, 1875 and 1888 plat maps.

Earhart Road where it not only intersects with Oxford Milford Road . . . but also where the living have been known to intersect with the dead.

Many years ago, two star-crossed lovers would meet on dark nights at the sharp veer where Oxford Milford Road and Earhart Road unite not far outside the town of Oxford. *She* would walk the Oxford Milford Road in Butler County, stopping at the exact spot the two roads merged. *He* would drive his motorcycle down the rural Preble County byways and pause on his motorcycle along Earhart Road. There, he would wait for the girl to signal three times that it was safe for him to come to her. Then, in return, he would signal three times with the headlight on his motorcycle to show he was there.

One night, her parents caught her sneaking from her home and she never made the walk along the quiet country road. He waited and waited and then infuriated, the young man raced down the roadway, failing to make the sharp turn. His motorcycle slid along the gravel edge, then flipped crazily into the air. When it finally made it back to the roadway, the bike came to a screeching halt in suddenly silent air.

He died that night on the roadway. But the young man still returns to search for his sweetheart. Those who park and have flashed their lights three times have seen the motorcycle headlight making a speedy run toward their car.

Legends say if you take this turn and pause with your car facing south (as if you just took this turn) and flash your headlights, a single headlight from the ghostly motorcycle will come chasing down the road toward you. However, be warned, it might be the local police who would certainly advise everyone of the dangers of stopping anywhere on the road.

Old Rossville Cemetery Ghost—Ten Foot Ghost

Early Rossville—1840s looking east toward the City of Hamilton. Image courtesy of the MidPointe Library System "Library Lens" Collection.

Rossville, Ohio was formed in 1804 as a separate entity, but close neighbor, to Hamilton. It had its own businesses and residential areas—breweries, drugstores, groceries and even its own cemetery located on the corner of Boudinot and Third streets, now Park Avenue and North D Street. But as time passed and the city of Hamilton grew, the residents of the smaller Rossville began to understand the value of uniting with their much larger neighbor. Besides, they already shared much of their community.

Six years before Rossville merged with Hamilton in 1854, Greenwood Cemetery was established. After the opening, Rossville residents were buried in this newer graveyard. And even 150 of the past burials for the old town were reinterred in Greenwood. However, the Rossville Cemetery (also called the Boudinot Cemetery) was still accepting burials until 1863.

Oh, and then a strange thing happened that would change the course of spiritual history for those bodies that had been laid to rest an eternity beneath this sacred ground in the old Rossville graveyard. Someone decided it was okay to simply plow right over them and make the old pioneer graveyard a city park. They did not gently remove those early settlers and rebury them in Greenwood. It was decided it would be much cheaper to cover the remaining bodies and headstones in the old pioneer graveyard of Rossville, numbering at least 215, with a foot and a half of soil and then, build the park over top them.

Rossville Cemetery after it became a city park. Only the indentations in the ground exposed, to the naked eye, the truth there was a cemetery buried beneath. Oh, and the ghosts that showed up at night. *Courtesy: Columbus Metro Library.*

A 1971 Hamilton Journal Newspaper would note that a single sheet of paper was inadvertently discovered in the Butler county archives among a box of miscellaneous papers that would show the fate of the graveyard—

> *"Hamilton, Ohio, June 13, 1878. Specification and Estimate for Burying the grave stones in the First Ward Park. Each head and foot stone must be buried on its respective grave with the lettered, side of the stone up and so that the top of the stone will be 18 inches below the surface of the ground. Estimated cost: Stones for 215 graves at 20 cents per grave. $43.00. Signed: John C. Weaver C.C.E."*

It would take ten years before the process of burying the cemetery below ground would begin. But in doing so, many of the graves were disturbed including the destruction of caskets and exposure of the bodies within. At one point, a local newspaper pointed out that neighborhood children had pried open several caskets that had been set aside during the building of the park and they were playing with the bones within. The year was 1888. And it was the same year something began stirring beneath the First Ward Park, something that had seemed to be building, raging, seething each time the already insulted ground was tauntingly poked with a shovel or plow. In fact, it was almost as if something beneath the soil was just waiting for that one last little jab to its freshly raw wound from the bully with the shovel to awaken the riled soul beneath. And so, in 1889, it would be:

> *What is claimed to be a genuine ghost has made its appearance in Hamilton, Ohio. The apparition has been seen in the old Boudinot burying ground in the First Ward, by a number of parties. About a year ago the grounds were put into the hands of the City Council, and an effort made to convert them into a park. The grand old trees that had stood for a century and shaded the tombs were cut down and the grave-mounds were leveled to the earth, the stones being carried away. The grave was robbed of its once solemn beauty and the hallowed associations of years disregarded. Day after day the graves were torn open by the plow and the ROTTING BONES Thrown promiscuously upon the ground. . .* ***Cincinnati Enquirer (Cincinnati, Ohio) July 27, 1890. A Ten-Foot Ghost Seen in the Old Boudinot Cemetery***

Rossville-1891 and about the same time the ghost appeared. Photograph courtesy of the MidPointe Library System "Library Lens" Collection.

It was a hot day, deep in the summer of 1890, the 24th of July. A plow working through the dirt of the new park had unearthed a tombstone bearing the inscription: "Charley, aged 12, son of Herman and Anna Carter." The curious in the close-knit neighborhood rushed to see the stone, ponder who young Charley had been. Those who were suspicious of riling the dead from their sleep began to whisper of repercussions from these long departed souls. Because surely, opening a grave must assuredly awaken the long-sleeping and cranky spirit beneath.

And then, it happened. It was three days later, Joseph Myers who lived across the street from the park on Boudinot Street was sitting in his doorway relaxing before he went to bed. He glanced up toward the park and blinked in surprise. Just a stone's throw away, he saw a shrouded figure arising from the disturbed resting place of young Charley Carter. This ghostly figure stood nearly ten feet tall and in its outstretched hands, a torch put out a brilliant light. Slowly, almost cautiously it floated through the park toward Boudinot Street. Joseph Myers arose with caution. Still, he was deeply fascinated. With the wary curiosity of a skeptic, he followed the tall figure for only a few moments. Then it disappeared completely into the dark night air.

However, the ghost was not quite finished. Others would see the apparition and tell their haunting tales. One such story came about a young man living on the other side of the park who boldly stated he would solve the mystery of the strange shrouded figure. He would prove it was nothing but bunk and certainly not the ghost of little Charley Carter coming back to haunt those who desecrated his grave.

So in the black of night, the brash young man situated himself within the bounds of the park. He waited quite patiently and a bit too smugly for the ghost to appear. And it would appear. It came at midnight. The ghost arose before the young man and perhaps not more than an arms-length away. The shrouded figure stood 10 feet above him and carried a bright torch that encompassed even the young man's shadow. It would be rumored later that the man was so badly frightened by the apparition that he bolted from his seat and did not stop running until he was twelve miles away in Reilly where he was found in a blackberry patch the next day.

The park still exists. It isn't called First Ward Park or Wayne Park anymore. It is Sutherland Park now, named for one of the area's early pioneers and donors of the cemetery land. The graves are still beneath. They get disturbed once in a while. City crews running gas lines through the grounds in 1964 unearthed a few graves. It happened again in 1994.

Then, Hamilton Park and Recreation employees accidently disturbed some stones and bones. For a while, there was even a small trench with 45 or so gravestones dumped haphazardly within. No one was sure to whom they belonged or even where they had once been initially placed to identify the body laying beneath.

But what of the ghost . . . should those who pass the park by night be afraid? Unless the graves are disturbed, you should be safe . . . almost certainly, that is, but not definitely. In saying this, perhaps it is suggested to tread lightly across the manicured lawn of Sutherland Park. And simply stay away after dark.

Old Rossville Cemetery Ghost—Dead Dancers

Sutherland Park. 1907. Where ghostly dancers were seen. From the Walter Havighurst Special Collections, Miami University Libraries, Oxford, Ohio.

Another ghost from the Rossville Cemetery, also called Boudinot Cemetery and now Sutherland Park, comes from long ago. In 1833, a cholera epidemic broke out in the City of Hamilton, Rossville and surrounding communities. Tainted drinking water from sewage was the usual culprit that instigated the disease. Common treatments of bleeding and purging did nothing to stop it. It was considered a fatal disease back then. And it was. One young woman was readying for her wedding but fell ill to cholera. On the day of her wedding, instead of walking up the aisle with her beloved sweetheart, she was buried in her wedding dress alone in the Rossville Cemetery.

People once saw ghostly dancers at Sutherland Park, eerie echoes of the land's grimmer past. From a unique ghost story retold by Jim Blount in the Journal-News (Hamilton, Ohio) May 11, 1994.

Distraught, her groom stood watch over her grave. Then, just a few days after his bride-to-be's death, he was found dead atop her headstone, a self-inflicted bullet in his head. For years, many would tell tales of seeing a bride and groom in full wedding attire dancing through the cemetery at dusk.

Legend of Hangman's Hollow

The road through Hangman's Hollow between Hamilton and Darrtown is known for a ghost story that had its beginnings during Butler County's first official fair in 1851.

On October 2nd and 3rd of 1851, Butler County held its first 'official' fair presented by the newly reorganized, state authorized Agricultural Society. It was set up in a small grove of oaks near the Miami-Erie Canal just north of Hamilton. There were no racetracks, no carnies selling games and certainly no 4-H kids displaying their projects. Instead, there were a small number of displays including samples of this year's summer harvests, farm implements, and live farm animals like horses, cattle and pigs.

A trip to the county fair for four local Darrtown boys turns into more than just a boyhood memory . . . it turns into a ghostly legend.

It wouldn't appear much by today's standards. But to four wide-eyed country boys between the ages of eight to twelve hailing from the small village of Darrtown, it was excitement enough to grab up their horses, saddle them up and head to Hamilton about nine miles away for the day. 12 year-old Taylor Marshall was the ringleader of the group. Along with him, rode 8 year-old Ben Scott, 10 year-old Chambers Flenner and 11 year-old Dan Warwick.

The boys enjoyed the day at the fair as kids will tend to do. As evening set on, they realized the road home would be getting quite dark as it was well into the autumn of the year. And the path they took was thick with forest, mile upon mile of trees and deep, dark hollows. Oh and there was one such place, the monster of them all as far as fearful places for young boys to travel through as darkness covers the sky. This one such place was the most dreaded of all and not just for young, superstitious boys with grand imaginations of ghosts and spooks and robbers. Along Darrtown Pike was a deeply secluded spot justly named Hangman's Hollow. Old records indicate it originally took its sinister-sounding name 22 years earlier in 1829, when on July 29th a Martin Koble from Lancaster, Pennsylvania hanged himself in this isolated pocket outside Hamilton.

A stranger, he was, and no one knew why he committed such a deed, but it took two years to even find his next of kin. And between then and the time the boys travelled through this little pocket of scary, it was a haven for thieves and ruffians and some thought, ghostly things.

Darrtown Pike in earlier, more remote days. It isn't difficult to imagine there were plenty of places between farms, then, for thieves to hide awaiting a carriage to pass. Photo Courtesy: Darrtown.com

You see, the road climbs a bit as you leave the city of Hamilton, then dips slightly and lazily down along an old ravine. It is hardly recognizable to drivers as anything more than a slight drop in the path. But to the right and left of the roadway when it slides downward, there is scrubby underbrush. Within a few steps, where it is easy for dark spooks or someone with the wrong deeds in mind to hide, a thin creek bed lays nearly hidden in the ravine.

So the boys dreaded the little section just outside the city. What is now only a short fifteen minute drive, with homes to left and right, would be a two to three hour secluded horseback ride back to Darrtown with Hangman's Hollow between the Butler County Fair and their cozy beds at home. So they started for home probably wishing they had left a little earlier in the day. The boys headed west out of the city along Darrtown Pike, now Hamilton Richmond Road. Then, it was heavily wooded with deep cuts and trees whose canopies were so thick, they would overhang the road, only making the path much blacker.

The boys made it to the top of the hill from town and about a mile and a half outside the town proper and began to descend slowly into the deep of the dreaded hollow. Dark, it was getting, but not quite black. The air was cool, October-like, and it got even cooler as they descended into the depths of the valley. It was then they heard soft whispers and ran into a small group of people stopped upon the roadway and staring into the dark woods beyond. They were talking quietly among each other, appeared quite pale and fearful.

Something was wrong on the roadway that night, something terribly amiss. For up on the ravine and not far off the roadway, something gruesome lay hanging there –

. . . Up the ravine not far removed from the road, a gruesome and a ghastly thing had been discovered. It was apparently the figure of a man who had committed suicide by hanging. Dismounting from their horses, the four young cavaliers at once investigated. With brave but hearts accelerated in their beating, they made their way up the dark recesses and some 50 to 75 feet from the pike they came upon the object of their search. It hung from a large root projecting over the run bed. The knees were resting on the ground with the body held upright by a pair of suspenders tied around the neck.

The features were blackened and distorted and hideous, and they had been pecked at and in part destroyed by the foulsome birds of the air and the insects of the wind . . . ***Hamilton Daily Republican News. (Hamilton, Ohio.) October 05, 1910. Legend of Hangman's Hollow. WIERD TALE IS RELATED AGAIN. An Early Incident of One of the Early Fairs***

Curious as boys are, the four dismounted and scurried along the hollow, following the pointing fingers through the archaic creek bed. It seems a farmer by the name of Jake Kelley searching for his lost pigs had come upon a body. And sure enough, there before them, a man was hanging with his suspenders around his neck.

Moaning Bridge of Hamilton

The Big Reservoir in Hamilton is haunted. Image circa 1900s.

By the late 1800s and early 1900s, Hamilton was a bustling city on both sides of the Miami River. There were a multitude of businesses—groceries and livery stables, watchmakers, paper companies, shoemakers, malt houses, and taverns. Yes, there is more to life than work so there were also plenty of places for recreation like the Butler County Fairgrounds, Krebs Ball Park, the Dixon-Globe Opera House and First Ward Park. And of course, among these places to idle away the hours were many locations for sweethearts to spend some time together, perhaps even for a short period, alone.

Big Reservoir: Circa 1907. From the Walter Havighurst Special Collections, Miami University Libraries, Oxford, Ohio.

One of those romantic locations was along what locals called the Big Reservoir. This reservoir was the large pool of stored backwater from the Great Miami that was used to run a hydraulic system that supplied water power to area mills and shops. It was also used for boating and swimming. At the head of this waterway, the Hamilton Club House rented out boats to paddle around the water during the summer.

Along the Big Reservoir, there were three wooden wagon bridges spanning the water. It was the third of these bridges, one located the farthest out from the club house where many young sweethearts would retreat. It was so low to the water, couples had to duck their heads to paddle beneath. But it was well worth the extra rowing. The remote setting was perfect for stealing a kiss and far away from prying eyes.

It was here along the backways of Big Reservoir that one such couple met. Many warm days of summer were spent rowing about the reservoir, chatting about their future together and sneaking a kiss now and then. They planned on being married soon, spending the rest of their lives together.

Big Reservoir: Circa 1906 with bridge in background. From the Walter Havighurst Special Collections, Miami University Libraries, Oxford, Ohio.

But fate would not give them this joy. Doctors informed the young man that he had the dreaded disease, consumption. And he only had a few weeks left to live. The knowing of death knocking at life's doorway can do foul things to muddy a man's mind. And such it did with this young man. His bride to be was beautiful and healthy. He refused to let another have her, refused to make her a widow. And so he took fate into his own hands. The 1889 Cincinnati Enquirer relates their horrible destiny best . . .

The two took their accustomed boat-ride one beautiful summer evening. They rode up to the bridge. Here, so far as could ever be learned, the young man deliberately shot his sweetheart through the head and then put a bullet in his own brain. The young lady did not die immediately, it is thought. And her head fell over one side of the boat, her golden cresses floating in the water. The boat was caught by an eddy and swung further under the bridge. A farmer passing over the bridge about that hour of the evening of the tragedy says he heard moans issuing from beneath the bridge and looked under it, but evidently did not see the boat. However, the boat slowly drifted down to the club-house. A crimson tide followed in its wake, the life blood of the fair young girl. The next morning early the boat with its ghastly burden was found at the club-house steps. The young lover could not live on earth with his bride. He would take her with him. ***Cincinnati Enquirer. (Cincinnati, Ohio) ProQuest Historical Newspapers. October 20, 1889. Pg. 20 The Moaning Bridge of Hamilton.***

The young man murdered his sweetheart, with a bullet to her head, then turned the gun upon himself. For years after their death, that last bridge along the Big Reservoir would moan in agony for the two sweethearts. Some would say it was nothing more than grasses. Others, the sound of water rippling through the rocks.

Frank Hums and Ellwood Mosey claim to have discovered the reservoir ghost, as they were swimming Tuesday night. Gliding down they found a spring gurgling up between two boulders of considerable size. When removed, the noise stopped. ***Hamilton Evening Journal. (Hamilton, Ohio) June 25, 1921.***

Big Reservoir: today.

And yes, perhaps the gurgling could explain some of the moaning and crying heard. But other ghostly occurrences have never been dispelled. Streaks of crimson are supposed to appear on the surface of the water between where the Moaning Bridge once stood and the Hamilton Club House. A ghostly boat has been seen floating with the current of water with its two dead sweethearts within. The young woman's golden hair trails along the water and the crimson glow of a red stream of her blood follows close behind.

Glowing Grave

The Glowing Monument

It was September of 1973 in the quiet farming community of St. Paris, Ohio when the peace of those eternally sleeping within the tiny Evergreen Cemetery was quite possibly shattered by a thousand footsteps above their graves. For almost a week, a continuous flow of onlookers flocked to the McMorran family marker at dusk to stand in awe of a glow emitted from the marble obelisk and embracing the graves around it. Local police literally had to put up barricades to stop the seemingly endless flood of as many as a thousand curiosity seekers a night. Explanations for the strange light ranged from luminescent mold or lighting to a spiritual message from God. Incidentally, Evergreen Cemetery was laid out in 1877 on property purchased by John McMorran whose grave lays among other family members beneath the glowing obelisk.

Lincoln Ghost Train

The Funeral Train for President Lincoln.

On April 21st of 1865, after President Lincoln had been assassinated, the nine car funeral train carrying his body weaved its way across the northern United States on its route toward Springfield, Illinois for burial. It made frequent stops along the way. And it wasn't simply to allow mourners to pay respects to the late president along the 13 day trip. Embalming of bodies was in its infancy. Stops were made often to freshen the flowers surrounding the body to keep the smell of rotting flesh to a minimum.

As the train progressed along its route, one of the places it trudged through was Urbana, Ohio on Saturday, April 29th at 10:40 p.m. Nearly 10,000 people showed up to see the train go by.

The train tracks as they appear today along a bike trail.

Nowadays, legends say that on April 29th a ghostly funeral car carrying the body of President Lincoln makes its way along the same tracks. On this special anniversary date, the train stopped briefly in 1865 where a depot once stood near North Main Street in Urbana. Some have seen it shrouded in black with a skeletal crew within while others have simply seen ghostly lights that vanish into nothingness. The spectral sound of the train's whistle sweeps along the track, and clocks throughout town are rumored to stop for 20 minutes, the same amount of time Lincoln's funeral train stopped in Urbana.

The closest designated parking area for the Simon Kenton Trail along the Rails-To-Trails corridor, which includes the section of track where the ghost train appears, is the Urbana Station Depot at 644 Miami Street (40.108998, -83.759710). It is about a 1/2 mile on a paved path and takes about ten minutes to walk. You will see the Lincoln train memorial plaque at your destination. There are also several local businesses closer to the site that may, with permission, allow you to park in their lots.

The Ghost Town of Sprucevale—Beaver Creek State Park

It started with a dream, a purchase of 300 acres along Little Beaver Creek, a stone gristmill and four brothers by the name of Hambleton—James, Charles, Benjamin and Isaac. That was 1813; by 1837, the Sandy and Beaver Canal was running right through the middle of their property and they laid out a town of nine lots between the creek and canal.

The town they called Sprucevale would grow large enough to boast a grist mill, pottery shop, woolen factory, general store, post office, warehouses, blacksmith shop and 12 homes. And so it lived well until around 1847 when the canal boom years waned with the coming of the railroad and the lack of funds to sustain it. So reliant was the town upon the canal that when it declined, the people and the buildings began to fade away too. By 1870, Sprucevale wasn't much more than a printed name on a map.

There is little remaining today but the Hambleton's stone grist mill, a bridge and the remnants of a few locks, all a little spooky and mysterious because we know people used them once, they are dead and gone and not coming back.

The only building left standing is the Hambleton Mill.

The ghost town of Sprucevale along the Sandy Beaver Canal.

What was a lively community is now barren and silent and not so far away from feeling like an old lonely cemetery. The leftovers of long dead villagers tease us like ghostly fingers wiggling in the air and beckoning those there to explore their past. And so someone has . . .

Jake's Lock—Located right in the park. It is named for a former caretaker along the canal who was struck by lightning while walking the canal one stormy night. His ghost strolls the lock with an oil lamp in hand. It is this flickering lantern light seen bobbing around at dusk.

The remnants of Jake's Lock.
GPS: 40.705821, -80.582400

Gretchen's Lock at Beaver Creek State Park.
GPS: 40.7078408, -80.593682

Gretchen's Lock—According to old archives, E.H. Gill was the chief canal engineer and a graduate of the Royal Engineer's School in Paris. He travelled from France along with his wife and seven year-old daughter, Gretchen, to help build the Sandy and Beaver Canal. Tragedy struck halfway to the United States when Gill's wife was washed overboard and was drowned. They had no choice but to bury her at sea. Grief-stricken, the father and daughter continued on to their new life.

Gill would get a job with the Sandy and Beaver Canal system and help in the building of the lock above Sprucevale. His daughter followed him from camp to camp, living in the wild area around the new canal. During this time, Gretchen contracted malaria. One afternoon as her fever mounted, she made her father promise to take her home and bury her with her mother—"I want to join my mother," she pleaded. Wanting to please her, the father nodded that certainly he would. Before the day ended, Gretchen was dead.

Gretchen's father temporarily entombed her in a cache in Lock 41 which is just above Sprucevale, a crypt which would bear her name. Gill would resign his position around 1837 and take a ship from Baltimore back to his homeland of France.

He removed Gretchen's casket from the lock and began his long journey home. On the return, a storm swept across the Atlantic Ocean near the Madiera Islands. It destroyed the ship and all its passengers and they were tossed into the ocean's depths. And as the young girl wished, she joined her mother in the sea.

> *. . . Little Gretchen was temporarily placed in a stone cache in Lock No. 41, just above Spruce Vale. On completion of the canal E. H. Gill, with the remains of his daughter, took ship from Baltimore for France. In a severe storm near the Madiera Islands, the ship foundered and all on board were lost. Thus was little Gretchen's request realized and she was "buried with her mother."* ***Ira F. Mansfield; Robin Hood Club. Little Beaver River valleys, Pennsylvania—Ohio with illustrated check list of flowers and essays. 1914***

But Gretchen isn't quite gone. Her ghost has been seen wandering the lock where she was once entombed and along the old Sandy and Beaver Canal in the town of Sprucevale.

> *. . . .At the canal lock below Vondergreen's, little Gretchen has often appeared murmuring her dying prayer "Bury me with my mother," . . .* ***Ira F. Mansfield; Robin Hood Club. Little Beaver River valleys, Pennsylvania -- Ohio with illustrated check list of flowers and essays. 1914***

For some reason, the tale of Esther Hale was elaborated in newer stories to include a beautiful bride and the bridge over Little Beaver Creek. In all my research, I could not find a shunned bride in the village nor any reference to the bride being Esther Hale who was actually a staunch Quaker preacher and well known among the canal workers at Hambleton Mill. The Spruceville Bridge at the mill was built in 1952. Regardless, the tale told here has references from genuine sources.

Esther Hale — The Quaker Preacher–

Ira Mansfield, author and historian, would recall Esther Hale as coming from the Carmel church of the Orthodox Friends. She was among the first of these robust Pennsylvania preachers, a hard worker who toiled among the laborers on the Sandy and Beaver Canal. She was a tough old bird, frugal and advised temperance among the rowdy canal men. Whenever Esther would preach, she would call out for those in her audience: "Follow me down the path to salvation!" Now on St. Nicholas's Eve, December 5th of each year, Preacher Hale appears at the old Hambleton grist mill dressed in white. She scratches "Come" on the wall of the old stone grist mill before she leads those watching inside and vanishes.

. . . in the deserted stone mill at Sprucevale, on St. Nicholas eve, the ghost of Esther Hale, the Quaker Lady preacher, appears and rewrites on the stone wall her old text "Come." Ira Mansfield; Robin Hood Club.Little Beaver River valleys, Pennsylvania —Ohio with illustrated check list of flowers and essays. 1914

In the cold throes of winter in 1902, the inhabitants of Salineville were haunted nightly by a ghost. It was on a lonely stretch of roadway aptly called Schoolhouse Hill where an old 6 room schoolhouse and church meeting place once stood.

It was not the typical ghost. Its appearance was different for each person who saw it and would even change from one night to the next—

The old schoolhouse on the hill. Courtesy: Cookie Sisco

Salinville Has a Genuine Ghost. Spook Hunters Out in Force-Visitor Has Many Queer Disguises

Salineville, O., Jan. 9.-A ghost with striking peculiarities, inhabits Schoolhouse hill, in this town, according to several citizens of unimpeachable veracity. For the past two weeks it has been seen nightly by those who were out late.

The remarkable fact about this apparition is that it appears in a different guise each time. Tom Ellis who has seen it twice says the first night it appeared as a tall, old man with a long beard, erect and walking briskly.

The next time it presented the same face, but seemed infirm, bent and decrepit and moved slowly with tottering steps. He got a good look at it as it was bright moonlight, but when within ten feet of him, the specter vanished as if the earth had swallowed it.

John Edge also saw the "spook." It was clothed in white and moving fast. To him it appeared as a headless man. Others describe it as having a youthful face, with a singularly horrible leer.

A number of courageous young men have formed a "ghost hunters' league" and propose to solve the mystery. ***The Stark County Democrat., (Canton, Ohio) January 13, 1903. Salineville Has A Genuine Ghost***

Pretty Boy Floyd Still Walks

The marker where Pretty Boy Floyd was killed.

Pretty Boy Floyd.

Charles Arthur Floyd, AKA "Pretty Boy Floyd" was an infamous bank robber during the 1930s. A poor farmer, he turned to a life of crime to escape the poverty of the depression. Although he was known for his violence during bank robberies, the destroying of mortgage papers at many of the banks he robbed made him popular in the public eye.

He had been hiding out for a year and most likely heading back to his home in Oklahoma when he was spotted in the nearby town of Wellsville. On October 22nd, 1934, he was then traced to the Conkle farm and gunned down in a cornfield by FBI agents. A plaque now stands where he was killed. But there is more than one sign to mark the place where he died. His ghost has been seen walking the roadway near his place of death.

The Lackawanna Ghost Train

Lackawanna Limited Train Wreck-1943. Image Courtesy: Carl L. Zimmer, Consultant: "Genealogy Research"

The Lackawanna Limited, a west-bound first class passenger train, was running late. It was speeding along an estimated 50 miles per hour down the track in Wayland, New York, a town about 4 1/2 hours west of New York City and about another four hour drive westward to Cleveland. It was 5:23 p.m on August 30th and it had 20 minutes lost time to make up. The 11 car train had 500 passengers, some of them were comfortably seated in Coach 6, the fifth passenger car in the line.

Among them were 9 year-old Betty Andrews from Nichols, New York and 23 year-old Virginia Kralek of Cleveland. There were also 16 women between the ages of 16 and 50, new recruits for the Woman's Land Army volunteers who helped harvest crops during World War II's shortage of farm help.

Lackawanna Limited Car 6 Interior

The boiler came to rest next to Car 6. Image Courtesy: Carl L. Zimmer, Consultant: "Genealogy Research"

Those within Car 6 would later state they were riding along smoothly until there was a terrible jolt.

The Lackawanna Limited had sideswiped a switcher freight engine that had not fully cleared the track. The Lackawanna Limited sheared off the front of the switcher and split the boiler. That very boiler came to rest alongside Car 6. It was then the boiler burst. Through the shattered car windows the explosion left behind, hot steam spewed into the car.

No. 3, a west-bound first-class passenger train, consisted of engine 1151, 1 mail-baggage car, 2 Pullman sleeping cars, 4 coaches, 1 dining car and 3 coaches, in the order named. . . This train passed Coshocton, 10.37 miles east of Wayland and the last open office, at 5:10 p.m., 9 minutes late, passed signal 3109, which displayed proceed, and while moving at an estimated speed of 50 miles per hour it collided with engine 1248.

Engine 1248 was derailed to the north and stopped upright and in line with the track. Steam and water connections were broken and the engine was otherwise badly damaged. . . The sixth car stopped against engine 1248, escaping steam and hot water from the engine entered this car and practically all the fatalities occurred therein. Interstate Commerce Commission. Investigation 2725. ***The Delaware, Lackawanna and Western Railroad Company. Wayland New York, August 30, 1943.***

Victims trapped inside the coach crouched beneath seats while water began to swirl two feet deep in the aisles and scald those within. Some died right where they sat. Others desperately climbed above the seats and smashed windows with hands and shoes to escape the deadly heat. The scent of burnt flesh filled the air along with the screams of those trying to get out. Neither little Betty nor Virginia got out alive. They would be two of the 27 victims who died in the wreck.

The bodies of the 27 victims were taken from the Lackawanna Limited car and laid to rest. Eventually it was repaired, the number on the car was changed from 6 to 62 and placed back into service for many years before it was retired again. Then, it somehow ended up at the Baltimore and Ohio train Roundhouse in Cleveland, saved from the scrapyard by the Midwest Railway Preservation Society that uses the old roundhouse to restore old train cars.

They painted it and put in newer windows (after the wreck, they still used the car but changed the number from 6 to 62 because no one wanted to ride in it). And it is here that the volunteers who give tours of the building and trains being renovated began to notice the ghosts. Steve Karpos, a society trustee, was a guide during one of the tours. At one such event, a guest kept noticing a period-dressed man standing in the rear. Believing it was a part of the tour, she raised a hand and asked Karpos when the other tour guide was going to speak. Karpos assured her there was no one else in the car but the tour group. At least not one that was among the living. Then, when the tour group walked outside people claimed to see a ghost sitting on the roof of the train car, legs dangling over the edge.

Steve Karpos, right, talks history, trains, and ghosts beside the haunted train car.

Steve Karpos gave us a tour of the Lackawanna Limited Car 6. He chuckled when he told us the story of the ghostly tour and then told us there have been voices and screams heard within when no one is there.

"There's a lot of ghosts in this car," Karpos said. "People that sat in here, when taking naps during work breaks, had their feet up on the chair and can feel something grabbing their legs. You open up the windows and the windows slam down on you. People see ghosts down at the rear end of the car in the evening. They hear a lady come screaming out of the woman's bathroom saying "Get out!"

We kept a voice recorder running to tape the interview with Mister Karpos, but didn't tell him later that when he was telling us about the lady screaming, "Get out!", she screamed right over his own words the exact same sentence. There was another blood-curdling scream on the tape, a voice telling us to "Stay home", and a man stating clearly "Say no to war." And there was a strange and low whistling like the sound of train brakes attempting to squeal to a stop.

So, haunted it is. The ghosts of the Lackawanna Limited's ill-fated Car 6 have come back to haunt the living. Karpos told us that the train may be leased out after it has its new makeover. Until then, they do offer tours in the Cleveland Flats about the trains coming into the roundhouse where they receive a new lease on life.

Old Hermit of Beck's Knob Road

Beck's Knob Road looking toward Allen Knob.

About six minutes along US 22 from downtown Lancaster and on Beck's Knob Road sits Shallenberger Nature Preserve. It is a quiet retreat for hikers. Trails lead upward to a high hill called Allen Knob and you can look out on the rolling hills and valleys below. If you were to stand here over a hundred years ago, you may have seen an old hermit who used to walk from Allen Knob (where he would spend his days reading his bible) along Beck's Knob Road, across the bridge of Hunter's Run and then to his home at the now privately owned Beck's Knob.

The old hermit walked this route each day. He is long gone, but you still may be able to see him march his lonely route from Allen Knob and along Beck's Knob Road. You see, the hermit died one night and asked to be buried in a grave he had dug on the bare edge of the knob where he loved to read. But his ghost has been seen walking the route along the roadway and to Hunter's Run Bridge like he did so many years ago.

The walk home each night for the old hermit was here along Beck's Knob Road across the creek called Hunter's Run and trudging toward Beck's Knob.

Clarksburg Ghost

The road to Clarksburg.

The defunct town of Clarksburg was named for Joshua Clark, an early settler in the region. It was only 2½ miles from Lancaster along Hamburg Road SW (not far from the Lancaster Country Club), and was also home to the Clarksburg Schoolhouse *and* the ghost that haunted it.

Now, the Clarksburg Schoolhouse is long gone. But in the late 1800s, it seems that a driver traveling along this once busy stagecoach route was murdered and his body buried near where the building stood. According to a local author—Herbert Turner in Fairfield County Remembered—thereafter, ghostly noises were heard in and around the building like the sound of a spirited stagecoach horse tromping his hooves and the tolls of a bell ringing. The murdered traveler was not the only ghost nearby. Along the roadway, a spooky black dog the size of a steer was noted by many who travelled there. It would follow carriage riders, and then vanish into thin air.

Delmont Murder

The old culvert on Delmont Road.

Fred Walker, Fairfield County farmer, heard screams one cold, snowy January evening of 1897 near his farm outside Lancaster. He asserted they came from the direction of the Hocking Township election house not far from what is now State Route 22 and Route 159, then Zanesville-Maysville Road. Not long after, the sound of hooves resonated in the air along the roadway. Whether Mr. Walker simply thought it was not worth investigating or he could find no source of the ruckus was never stated. The sounds were simply cast aside as perhaps the cry of a spooked horse or the whine of a pig on a cold winter night. So, more snows of winter would cover the ground and the memory faded away.

Well, until a couple months later. It would be a mild March day with a pleasant southerly wind flow and a bit of sun peeking out through clouds that thawed the snow and revealed the man who made those screams. You see, those cries must surely had been his last. John Daugherty, foreman for the Cincinnati and Muskingum Valley Railroad found a lifeless, decomposing corpse in the mucky culvert near the train tracks and roadway. The dead man was described as well-dressed and middle-aged. His throat was slashed from ear to ear. No one recognized the stranger. Most assumed he was a salesman who was making his way from town to town along the busy highway. He had been robbed and murdered and left to rot on the cold, winter ground.

Gone, the Delmont murder victim may be. But his ghostly form with gaping wound was once a steady sight walking along the roadway in winter. Carriage riders and even later, car drivers would see the mystery man walking from Delmont Road to the culvert on State Route 159, a full-bodied apparition that then disappeared suddenly as a hazy mist into the ditch.

Weeping Lady

This photo showing the ghostly lady in the background was taken at the bridge by Brian Smith. Tammy Smith and her son Jaron are in the foreground.

The bridge stands over Clear Creek, still tall and proud like it doesn't realize carriage and car traffic no longer moves within its wooden walls.

The Johnston Covered Bridge was built in 1887, and until the early 1990s, could still handle the heavy weight of cars. Now it is only open to foot traffic . . . and the occasional ghost. Local lore tells of a weeping woman who is seen within its walls. The ghost has been spotted pacing back and forth along the bridge or peering out of one end as if she is waiting for someone to meet her. Two local legends are pinned to her—one is that she was a woman scorned by her husband and hung herself from the top bridge supports. The second story tells of a woman who jumped from her carriage during a terrible storm, only to fall into the swollen creek water below and drown.

Shimp's Hill
Ohio 158 (Lancaster-Kirkersville Road NW)
Lancaster, Ohio 43130
39.762406, -82.617337

Headless Man of Shimp's Hill

Shimp's Hill.

It was in the wee years of Fairfield County's history and about 1818 when George Shimp settled on 88 acres of land in Greenfield Township four miles from Lancaster. Along the northwest section of his property, there was a well-used road travelers took between the city of Lancaster and outlying communities like Dumontsville and Baltimore. And it was here that the road made a large, c-shaped veer, for there was a steep hill with a difficult summit to pass that was right in the path of travelers. The hill would be dubbed "Shimp's Hill" for the owner of the land. In the 1860s, Shimp's Hill was graded at its steepest part, and a cut was made through the hill for a more direct and safer route.

Some time during its early years, a man traveling near the summit of Shimp's Hill was not only robbed and murdered, but his head was taken from his body. Old timers still spoke in the early 1950s that the ghost of the man could be seen staggering around the hill searching for his head.

Has No Head

In mid-November of 1894, a 54 year-old wine agent for Brandt and Company in Toledo by the name of Albert Dittelbach was visiting the city of Columbus for business. Those around him noticed he was rather downcast, but no one expected to find him dead in the popular Schiller Park in German Village. He had committed suicide by shooting himself in the head.

The German Albert Dittelbach shot himself in Columbus, Ohio on Tuesday afternoon in front of the Schiller monument in the city park. The suicidal man came three months ago from Toledo to Columbus as an agent for the "Brand Wine Company", however business was not going well, his money depleted, and in the end even his lodgings were cancelled. On Friday afternoon he went into "Kings guesthouse" (bar) , drank a glass of beer, lit a cigar, and left with the words:" Now I am going to shoot myself". Of course the present people thought it to be a bad joke. For him it was absolutely serious. Around 5 o'clock (5pm) a few boys that were playing in the city park heard a shot from the direction of the Schiller monument, ran there and found Dittelbach laying on the foot of the monument inside the enclosure. He aimed well; the bullet went through his mouth into his brain, and he must have died immediately. A brother of the deceased lives in Texas. Dittelbach was about 55 years old and not married. ***Der Deutsche Correspondent., November 19, 1894. Translated by Margit Chevalier.***

Schiller Park 1908—Courtesy: Columbus Metro Library.

On Friday November 30th and less than two weeks after Dittelbach's death, two young men – William Bell and a friend– were returning from a party and took a short-cut through the dark, deserted park. They would wish they had not. Just within the bounds of the park, they noticed a figure draped in a gray robe from shoulders to knees. He was pacing back and forth with hands outstretched along the walkway directly in front of the Schiller Monument. Curious, the two paused to take in the lone stranger. To their horror, they saw he had no head.

HAS NO HEAD. A Real Ghost Cavorting About the Columbus City Park. Columbus, Ohio. *December 4.-A ghost is said to be haunting the City Park, and great excitement prevails on the South Side. Among a large number of persons who claim to have seen the supernatural being are William Bell and a young man named Sedinger. They say that when returning home from a party last Friday night they took a short cut through the City Park. Just south of the Schiller monument they saw the figure of a man walking with outstretched hands slowly to and fro in the driveway in front of the monument. The glare of an electric light a few hundred feet distant enabled them to see the figure distinctly, and suddenly Sedinger grasped Bell by the arm and said: "See, he ain't got any head."*

Cincinnati Enquirer (Cincinnati, Ohio) December 5, 1894 page 4.

. . . While the badly frightened young men were consulting, the figure continued to walk to and fro, its arms extended as if imploring aid. The figure was draped from the shoulders to the knees in a grayish cloak or robe, which added to its ghostly appearance. They looked closely, but not a sign of a head could be seen. They decided it was a ghost, and a headless one at that, and they lost no time in getting off the grounds. They said nothing about their adventure next day for fear of being laughed at, but Sunday they happened to meet some friends who reside near the park, some of who were telling about having seen the identical ghost they had seen, and under much the same circumstances. Albert Dittleback, a Socialist, and a stranger in the city, committed suicide by shooting himself in the mouth just at the spot where the ghost is said to have been seen. It is the theory of the superstitious South Side people that the ghost is Dittleback's spirit returned. ***Cincinnati Enquirer December 5, 1894 page 4.***

Schiller Park, where the ghost was seen at the monument, has about the same look today as it did back in the 1800s when it was called Stewart's Grove, then City Park.
This statue was added in 1891.

Nowadays, a few people take a morning jog along the sidewalks on the outskirts of this quiet park in German Village. Others may walk in the evening past the Schiller monument for a quiet respite from their busy day. No one has seemed to complain about a ghostly visitor for years. The story has been lost to time. Yet, you have to wonder if anyone passing by at night time, when the headless ghost of Albert Dittelbach was said to walk to and fro in front of the statue, has seen his shadowy figure and simply not known what they were seeing!

Little Ghost in Dublin

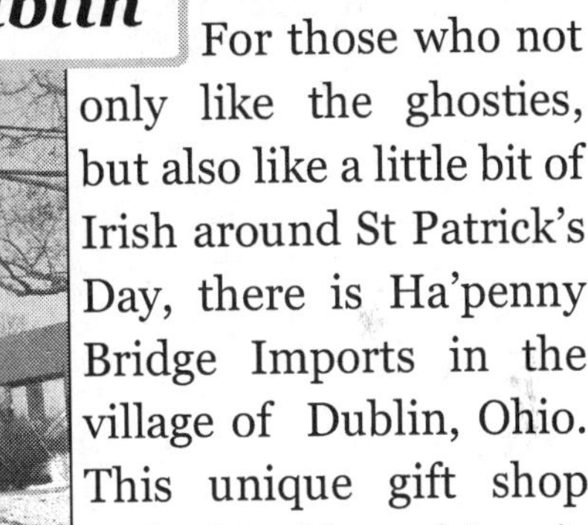

For those who not only like the ghosties, but also like a little bit of Irish around St Patrick's Day, there is Ha'penny Bridge Imports in the village of Dublin, Ohio. This unique gift shop tucked inside an historic home has everything Irish you can think of including Irish Wishing Stones, t-shirts, bagpipe kits and kilts. Oh, did I forget to mention they also have a little ghost?

Co-owner of the shop, Anne Gleine has an excited sparkle to her eyes when she talks of the dolls in the shop and how they might hold some interest to a little ghost that must have lived in the home. A China doll sitting on a shelf was found standing upright on the floor, completely unbroken. And other dolls within the shop are found mysteriously moved from one place to another. A tiny, bright room near what was once the living area seems to hold the key to the mysterious little visitor. Perhaps within those walls, a little girl once played. Now she plays mischievous tricks, like a little Leprechaun, on the owners!

Old Maid

The Old Governor's Mansion has seen many inhabitants since its beginnings as the Lindenberg family home in 1904. It was home to ten Ohio governors beginning in 1919 and then became a restaurant in the 1970s. Since 1988, it has housed The Columbus Foundation, a community improvement foundation. And yes, by the way, this regal old building has even shared its rooms with ghosts.

From 1977 to 1981, the Mansion Restaurant made its home in the building. During this time, a manager who was talking on the phone in her office saw an unfamiliar black woman dressed in what appeared to be a blue maid's uniform pass by her doorway. When the manager arose to investigate, the woman had disappeared. After that, staff were said to see the same ghostly figure around the rooms and near the main stairway. A face has even been seen looking out of the windows by people passing by along Broad Street. But that isn't all. The fetid scent of burning hair has filled the air within the rooms and pictures have been known to strangely fall from the walls.

The Road Near The Old Holverstott Place

Fairground Road
Xenia, Ohio 45385
39.735800, -83.974399 to
39.735973, -83.976137

Scared at a Ghost on the Road

The very slight step which often intervenes between supreme happiness and crushing sorrow, was awfully illustrated on last Friday, a few miles from Xenia, Ohio. Joseph Wolf was recently married, and had just returned from his wedding trip, and rented a piece of ground which he began to farm. . .

A reporter from The Jackson Standard wrote this on August 27th, 1885. His words could not be truer. Joseph Wolf was just 21 years-old, only two weeks married and fresh from his honeymoon when a simple twist of fate sent him walking blindly and straight onto the wrong path. Only one step in the opposite direction would have changed his life.

Quiet and hardworking, Joseph had just rented a piece of land for himself and his bride, and he was eager to get started with his life. Along with his little brother, 15 year -old Walter, he had gone out in the evening to begin plowing this new little farm. Beside the two young men, a playful pup had followed not far behind, dashing amidst a gaggle of lazy geese grazing in the grass

It would be this pup that would lead young Joseph on his ill-fated trip, for it wasn't long before something far more inviting caught his attention. In a blink of an eye, while Joseph and Walter were distracted by the plow and enjoying each other's company, the pup went tearing down the roadway toward the property of a gruff 62 year-old neighbor, George Halverstott, who was sitting on his porch. His prized turkeys, the pup's newest interest, were wandering around his lawn.

In playful freak the dog chased some turkeys belonging to a man named George Holverstatt, who came out with a double-barreled shotgun, with the avowed intention of shooting the dog. Some disputing followed between the men, Wolf started toward Holverstatt, and the latter fired one barrel at his breast, tearing a frightful wound. The shooter then attempted to fire the other barrel, but Wolf caught the weapon. Wolf died in a few minutes and the assailant gave himself up. . .
The Jackson Standard., (Jackson C.H.,Ohio) August 27, 1885.

George Holverstott grabbed his gun just as Joseph Wolf came to the pup's side and an angry dispute of words between the two began. Quite possibly, Joseph stepped forward to protect the pup just as Holverstott aimed and fired his double-barrel shotgun. The shot aimed true. . . but at the man and not the pup, tearing a whole into Joseph's chest. The young man, wounded and terrified, had rushed toward the old man crying, "My God, don't shoot me again!"

But the old man did shoot even as Joseph caught the weapon and tried to seize it from Holverstott's grasp. At that point, Joseph turned to his brother and sent Walter on the half mile run to get their mother. But less than ten minutes after his mother and new bride arrived and fell to his side, Joseph Wolf died in their arms.

But the story didn't end there. History has taught that with great tragedies come lives unfinished and, such, the likelihood of ghosts. And so it would be in one farming community in Greene County. It was not long before a spirit began to show its face around the roadways near the murder site—

SCARED AT A GHOST

An apparition Appears in the Woods Near the Scene of the Holverstott-Wolf Murder.

*We are in receipt of a communication to the effect that the people of the vicinity of the Holverstott-Wolf murder are frequently frightened by a fearful apparition that appears in the woods along the road where the murderer Holverstott lived. It is said to frighten men, women and children, and horses and assumes as some assert, the form of "the old imp himself," and some say the "image of another," and others allege one of "a hellish crew." Some measures for the capture of the ghost or fiend, whichever it is, are going to be made according to the informant. It is further stated that some anonymous papers have been written and circulated in the neighborhood that are causing a great deal of feeling and the murder of Joseph Wolf seems not likely to be forgotten very soon. The scene where the bloody deed was committed is unceasingly visited and everyone who passes there, especially at night and at dusk, is filled with a peculiar dread—**News Gazette-Springfield Globe-Republic., (Springfield, Ohio) March 16, 1886. Scared at a Ghost***

And the March 20th, 1886 Cleveland Plain Dealer was one of the first to pick up this local story and report it around the state:

People in the vicinity of the Holverscott-Wolf murder, near Xenia, are, in the woods frightened by an apparition that appears.

George Holverstott was arrested, indicted for murder and found guilty. He was sentenced to life in prison. He was later pardoned after 20 years in 1906 and was set free on Thanksgiving of that year.

Joseph Wolf was buried in a quiet little cemetery behind Byron Church. His ghost may not be there among the headstones, but perhaps those driving along the backroads of Greene County see him once in a while, but can't quiet pinpoint who or what they saw. Still, he has no worries. Visitors to the graveyard won't need his spirit around to let them know his story. Along one side of his monument, etched into the stone, it clearly states: *Killed by George Holverstott.*

Legend of Fiddler's Green

On certain nights, a green light can be seen floating up along the tombstones of Darby-Lee Cemetery in Cincinnati. The sound of a fiddle playing faraway blends with the leaves shivering in the breeze while its eerie echo slips along the green grass nearly hiding the aged graves . . .

Darby-Lee Cemetery is tucked into the woodland overlooking the Ohio River in Delhi Township of Cincinnati. It is small, protected by an aged wooden fence and has about 17 ancient gravestones surrounding a pale obelisk in the center.

Darby Lee Cemetery sits atop a hillside overlooking the Ohio River to the left of the picture. A ghostly lantern bobbing in the woods has been seen there. The strange sound of a fiddle has woven its way through the woods long after the fiddler has been dead.

This center monument, grayed with age, belongs to the landowner, a man by the name of Henry Darby (1781-1852) who was also an avid abolitionist. During the early 1800s, Mister Darby would walk to the tall hill that overlooked the Ohio River below, light his lantern and play his fiddle to signal safety to the escaping slaves crossing over the river from Kentucky. Not long after he died and was buried at the very place he summoned so many to safety, people began to see the glow of his lantern bobbing around the cemetery. They would hear the ghostly, shrill sounds of his fiddle sweeping between the hills and down to the river, still beckoning to those below it was safe to cross.

The Ghost of Mary Cunningham

Are there really ghosts? This was the big question running rampant in Cincinnati in the early spring of 1889. The curious whispers worked their way down brick streets and dirt alleys like tendrils of smoke weave their way upward and through the closed hallways of an old building whose basement has caught fire. Five people saw the ghost of a dead woman. *Is it true? Is it only their imagination?* It started about a half block down from Linn Street just off West Court Street on a cozy backstreet of brick apartments along a place called Hand Alley. The approximate point was just a little ways along the alley from Clark Street where there once stood the apartment known as 2 Hand Alley.

2 Hand Alley. It was the place Mary Cunningham died on the miserably chilly day of December 30th, 1888. She was only 30 years old and suffered. Her death certificate stated the reason for her passing was phthisis pulmonalis. It is more commonly called tuberculosis today. By her side was her much-beloved 13 year-old daughter named Anna and her mother, Mrs. Meany. Another was a young neighbor by the name of Katie Cline who helped nurse the woman during the sickness, too.

It was upon her death bed and in a delirium, Mary Cunningham threatened those around her: “If you do not care for my daughter, I will come back to haunt you!” Little was thought of the threat; the sick woman was hysterical. But on Thursday, March 28th, 1889 and less than three months later, the ghost of Mary Cunningham returned to eke out her vengeance upon those who had heard those very words.

She came to them in the night, as spirits tend to do. The ghost of Mary Cunningham would first frighten a relative of the Clines who lived on Gorman Street and was returning from the grocery. The ghost passed the woman swiftly, but she did not hide her features. So much was the woman startled by the ghost, she became hysterical and fell quite ill.

Three days later, Katie Cline and her sister, Alice, were sitting on the steps of their porch on 6 Hand Alley along with two young gentlemen and at the tail end of a date. It was 10 o’clock at night. They were chattering lightly about the evening beneath the light of the street lamp when a shadow slithered by, then stopped.

The Cincinnati Enquirer described the ghostly scene like this:

"KATE, WHERE IS MY ANNIE?"

This startling scene transpired about ten o'clock Thursday night. The two ladies were the Misses Alice and Kate Cline, sisters , who with their escorts, having just returned from some entertainment, were standing on the stone steps of the Cline residence, No. 6 Hand street, a small thoroughfare running north from Court street, just east of Linn street. The two couples were resting on the steps a moment before bidding each other good night when the form of a woman passed in front of them and turning to the left

WENT INTO AN ENTRY

Between No. 6 and the adjoining building. The shadow, or whatever it was, almost immediately returned, and stopping in front of the younger of the sisters, slightly pushing back a shawl which the apparition wore over her head, so that its features stood clearly revealed, addressed her very distinctly and with a touch of pathos in her voice: "Katie, have you seen any thing of my daughter Annie?" With a hysterical gasp Miss Cline, to whom the words were addressed, reeled backward against the doorstep and

FELL FAINTING

Into the arms of her escort. The other young lady was also overcome with the shock, and exclaiming "My God!" "My God!" fell against her sister. The wraith slowly receded and quickly disappeared into the darkness, although immediately in front of where the young people stood was a lamp-post which clearly revealed the ghost. . . ***Cincinnati Enquirer (Cincinnati, Ohio) April 1, 1889 Page 8. A REAL GHOST.***

The ghost came upon them. So quiet were her steps, no one heard it until it stood in front of the two couples. Both the young women and one young man recognized the spirit immediately as the dead Mary Cunningham. She wore a small plaid shoulder shawl over her head and her hands were concealed into the folds of her garments. Only when she pushed her shawl back could they see the face of the wraith bathed in the light of the street lamp. "KATE, WHERE IS MY ANNIE?" she asked and vanished into the shadows. Both girls fainted dead away.

The two young women recovered from their shock. There were never any findings that Anna was treated badly by her grandmother with whom she stayed thereafter. Still, people tiptoed around the alley for a long time after hoping they would not see the spirit.

Nowadays, quiet walkways and apartment stoops don the same pathways the ghost took well over 125 years ago. It doesn't seem like a scary place at all. Kids play between the brick flats and cars instead of carriages fill the streets. Laughter and the scent of grilling hamburgers slip along where the old alley stood. A horn honks and a dog barks along the roadway. And the ghost of Mary Cunningham stays hidden from the eyes of the modern world. At least, as far as we know.

John Scott Harrison Walks the Graves

The cemetery overlooking the Ohio River in North Bend was on land once owned by the family of President William Henry Harrison and the founder of the village of North Bend, John Symmes. It is about 16 miles from Cincinnati, along the river and sitting atop a steep hill. In Harrison's day, it was called "The Pasture Graveyard" and was mainly used by the Symmes and Harrison families. After the Civil War, it was renamed Congress Green.

73 year-old John Scott Harrison was once buried in this cemetery. He bears the distinction of being the only man who was both the parent (Benjamin Harrison) and child (William Henry Harrison) of U.S. presidents. However, he would become better known for something most horrific occurring right after his death.

The Harrison family plot at Congress Green.

On May 25th, 1878 John Scott Harrison died suddenly on his estate "The Point Farm" near North Bend. He was buried in the Congress Green Cemetery at the Harrison family plot in a grave on the rolling hillside. On the day of the services, his son, Benjamin, was walking the cemetery with his brother, John Jr., and George Eaton, a grandson of John Scott Harrison. The men were shocked to find the grave of 23 year-old Augustus "Gus" Devin, who had died only a week before on May 18th, disturbed. The casket had been broken and tossed back into the partially covered grave.

Body snatchers. They knew it the moment it was examined. Grave robbing by medical schools was quite common in the 1800s. Digging up fresh cadavers was a means to make some cash by those without conscience. It was a cheap way for colleges to obtain bodies to study.

In fact, schools held contracts with companies that would collect bodies for dissection and anatomical demonstration. It was part of the agreement between these companies and the medical colleges, no corpse would be taken from private burial grounds. It was common practice for the contractors to cut the ceratoid artery, inject the arteries with a preservative and cut the beard from the face. The body, then, became quite unrecognizable to even family members. So no one would recognize if the body was taken from private property or not.

It was a lucrative business of buying and selling dead bodies. The medical colleges seldom asked where the bodies had been obtained. They knew their contractors got most cadavers from freshly buried graves. However, it was certainly an unexpected shock for those who found the opened grave of Augustus that day. He was a personal friend of both John Jr. and George Eaton.

Hoping to bring the body snatchers to justice and keep his dead father and others safe from more body snatching, the three men began investigating the crime. In the meantime, Benjamin and his brother, John Jr. attempted in every way to make sure their father's body was not stolen. The grave was excavated eight feet and surrounded by a cemented brick vault. Dirt used to fill it was mixed with heavy stones and chunks of marble. Night watchmen were hired to watch the grave.

Benjamin Harrison, sure his father was safe from grave robbers, returned to his work in Indiana. It would be John Jr. and George Eaton who continued the search for the body of Augustus Devin. They obtained search warrants to inspect the medical schools in the area to find their friend and began working their way from one to the next. Upon entering the Ohio Medical School on Sixth Street in Cincinnati with Constable Walter Lacy and local police, they were escorted by a janitor from room to room throughout the building. They found nothing pertaining to Augustus.

It was not until they were about to leave, they found a trap door with an attached rope. One of the policemen seized the crank to open it and pull the rope upward. Ten minutes of turning brought the rope to the floor level with a naked, pale cadaver swinging attached. The arms were crossed and the rope was fastened around the body's midsection. A cloth covered the head, but a swatch of gray hair showed from beneath. Not only was the man elderly, but he was much larger than Augustus who had been emaciated at death due to consumption. Dismayed they had not found their friend, John Jr. declared that they should let the corpse back into the pit. They were just about to return the body into the vault when Constable Lacy removed the cover from the man's head. To the utter horror of John Jr., the corpse belonged to his own father!

Much fanfare was made of the discovery in newspapers. The corrupt ways some medical schools collected bodies were brought to light. In December 1879, the body of John Scott Harrison was reinterred without ceremony in the grandiose Harrison family tomb adjacent to Congress Green, safely locked in cement building and behind a wrought iron gate.

John Scott Harrison was reburied in a new tomb at the Harrison vault adjacent to Congress Green.

You can visit his grave, peer between the bars to the tomb and see where he was reburied. But you can't get too close and for good reason. However, you may see his ghost. The spirit of John Scott Harrison has been seen walking among the graves at Congress Green. There have also been stories of a man dressed in civil war attire standing next to graves, mists and lights, and the sounds of children's voices talking.

Ghosts of Dola Marsh

The region around Dola Marsh is fertile farm field for as far as the eye can see.

Hog Creek Marsh was located between Ada and Dola, Ohio along the tiny Hog Creek. The land here was once a shallow, marshy lake lush with cranberries, wild grasses and many little animals flourishing within. However in 1868, the land was dredged to drain away the water for farming of soybean and corn.

Old-timers used to say that the little animals left without homes and food after the draining would come back once a year to haunt the farmers there. Their ghosts would peer into windows, eyes glowing and their little nails would make a tap-tap-tapping sound on the windows of homes nearby. At midnight on Halloween, the Wyandot Indians would ride along the edge of the swamp where they spent more than fifty years after battling General Anthony Wayne in 1794. They, too, were tossed off the land in July of 1843. They disappear into the rows of corn and build tall shocks to remind those of Dola of the homes they had to leave.

A Weird Tale in Providence

Ohio once had a series of locks along the Miami and Erie Canal system by the Maumee River near Grand Rapids at a now defunct canal boomtown called Providence. One section where boats could come in along the slack waters of Providence Dam of the river was a guard lock called Buckland's Lock. Here, boats from the Gilead Canal, which was across the Maumee River, could lock into the Miami and Erie Canal. Then they could work through a series of locks including Lock 44.

Seasonally these days, some of the canal and locks have been rebuilt and visitors to Providence Metropark just outside the town of Grand Rapids can take a mule-drawn boat ride along the calm waters of the canal. It is a fun and laid-back scenic family trip. But it wasn't always so pleasurable and easy-going as was mentioned in a 1902 article in the Akron Daily Democrat:

Napoleon, O., July 21-Nestled in a clump of trees, almost on the boundary line between Lucas and Henry counties, is a famous landmark on the Miami and Erie canal, called Buckland's Locks, and around this spot is woven a weird tale of tragic mystery which has lately culminated in a series of the strangest happenings in the history of the canal. . . . Boatmen passing the spot after dark, are startled by weird groans, near the shore, as though some one was in great agony. But instead of growing fainter the cries increase, until suddenly a misty figure rises apparently from the water just in front of the boat, as it pauses near the lock. The form can be plainly seen and is that of an old man, who fumbles about the sluice gates ahead of the craft a moment. Then stepping back, he throws them open and without a word, fades away. As the boat continues its course to pass through the locks, the bargemen to their amazement see that the gates are tightly closed, although they could have sworn that the mysterious man of the night had opened them for them a moment before. At the second lock the strange figure is again seen, and so on until the series is passed, each time repeating the performance. . . ***Akron Daily Democrat. (Akron, Ohio) July 21, 1902, Page 5. A Weird Tale of the Canal Locks Near Napoleon***

During the 1800s, as canal boatmen neared the Buckland Lock, they would hear cries and groans along the shoreline as if someone was in great pain. Louder it would get, until a mist would rise from the canal waters before their boat. Then the mist would form into a clear, gaunt figure of a little old man. He would fumble around the sluice gates before stepping back and opening them wide.

Buckland Lock is located on a gravel pull-off on Hwy 24 2.3 miles southwest of Providence Metropark.

Such the boats would begin to pass through the lock only to find out the gate was not opened at all. This would happen at each of the series of locks running this section of the canal, the old misty ghost reappearing and disappearing at each gate to the shock and amazement of the boatmen.

It seems the previous keeper of the locks at Providence during the 1880s was a heavy-drinking man by the name of Bill Bellington. Near midnight one fateful day after he had been drinking heavily, the cry of alarm was let out that his quarters were on fire. The next day, his charred body was found within. Many believe he was murdered for the money rumored to be hidden within his home. For years after his death, the little old man's ghost was seen at Buckland's Lock and Lock 44, a spirited presence to boatmen and others along the canal.

Even now, you can walk the Towpath Trail at Providence Metroparks, working your way along the old Buckland's Locks. And you can even take a step back in time and enjoy a mule-drawn canal boat ride seasonally at the park. While you're there, keep your eyes peeled for a mist around the locks, then the ghostly figure of old lock keeper Bill Bellington fumbling with the gates.

Capering Imp of Darkness

Dunn's Chapel and Cemetery to right. Anderson Road where the farmer traveled.

On August 30th of 1888, a farmer related a story to the News Herald in Highland County. While traveling west along Anderson Road about five miles from Hillsboro around midnight, the farmer had just passed Dunn's Chapel and the tiny graveyard behind. Hearing a low groan-like snarl to his right, he paused curiously. Turning his attention to the headstones, the man spotted a peculiar white object moving among the graves. Believing it might be a dog or calf, the farmer whistled shrilly. To his disbelief, the white creature made a guttural growl, sprang over the churchyard fence and tore across the grassy meadow toward him.

He looked on, horrified, watching as it cleared the fence and two furry white sheets resembling wings drew up from its sides.

The farmer was frozen to the spot for as long as it took for the strange dragon-like ghost to circle him three or four times. The beastly creature of darkness, as he would call it, used its wings after and bound huge strides back and forth. Swiftly coming to his senses, the farmer mustered enough sense to dig out his pocket knife and take a few small steps forward. The creature crouched as if to spring at the farmer, whipped his tail back and forth and let its wings flap into the air.

. . .When within a few feet of me the monster stopped and commenced circling around me, lashing its great slender tail from side to side and alternatively raising and lowering its white wings, which seemed to come out at the shoulders and extend along its back to its tail. I could see its eyeballs flashing yellow gleams of light and its wide mouth displaying rows of fierce white teeth. It seemed to be about as large as a good-sized dog, but its fore legs were twice as long as its hind legs, and its head and fore shoulders were three times as large as all the rest of the body. Its body seemed to taper off to a tail with two short legs attached behind, and as it half walked and half hopped around me I could see the whole body to good advantage. . . ***The News-Herald., September 06, 1888. What Is It? What An Honest Farmer Saw at Midnight in a Country Graveyard.***

One step at a time, the terrified farmer moved forward with the wraith taunting every footfall until he reached a small bridge at the end of the chapel and graveyard property. There the beastly creature made a large swoop and stopped directly in front of the man on brown-legged haunches. He showed sharp teeth and growled.

Dunn's Chapel and the dark woods beyond.

The farmer cringed inwardly when he realized that he was now positioned where the dark woods beyond Dunn's Chapel seemed to swallow up any pale light the stars in the almost-black sky gave out. His eyes played tricks on him—the trees danced like ghosts, branches like arms reaching out to grab him. It was here he was most vulnerable. Then, unexpectedly, a neighbor's dogs began to bark. Without warning, the creature tore away into the woods and disappeared from sight.

The farmer crept home through the fields past Dunn's Chapel and most likely peered quite often over his shoulder, feeling like a miserable ball of fear. So what was this wraith-like beast digging around in the graveyard? We may never know. The next morning, the shaken farmer returned. On one grave, there were several rake marks. And he found upon the road tracks that looked like a huge chicken had been walking around with a forked claw to each toe.

Fallsville Ghost

The road leading to Fallsville, Mill Street. The Clouser homestead was on the left. Only foundations remain.

You might spend Christmas Eve sitting in front of the TV with a cup of eggnog watching old black and white holiday movies. Or maybe you'll go to a candlelight church service or shop for last minute gifts. These are all typical American holiday traditions. But you may not know this—a traditional Christmas in Victorian England was held around the fire at night telling the most horrifyingly morbid of ghost stories. You see, December 25th was set aside for Christmas because of the Pagan festivals centered around Winter solstice, the shortest and most haunted day of the year.

On this day of mostly darkness, the walls between the living and dead were lowered so that the spirits could come through. Hence, the popularity of ghostly tales of years past like the Charles Dicken's classic *A Christmas Carol.*

So. . . in celebration of those old-time traditions, here is a timeworn ghost story you can tell around your own fire next Christmas. And perhaps, any time of the year, you can walk the same paths those who are in the story walked long ago, maybe see the strange things they had seen. It happened over 150 years ago in the tiny town of Fallsville which is now Ohio Division of Wildlife's Fallsville Wildlife area. It was about a ghost that would show up on the front lane of a quiet little homestead and scare one family each Christmas Eve.

Simon and Elizabeth Clouser and their three children – Charlotte, Susanah and Samuel moved into a home along Falls Lane in the tiny town of Fallsville, Ohio in the early 1800s. It was a small farming community settled around the waterfalls of Clear Creek in Highland County. Simon was the local miller in the mid-1800s, his job entailing grinding up the local corn and wheat into meal or flour for his customers. His stone house and gristmill were located along the cascading waterfalls of Clear Creek.

The Falls of Clear Creek where the Clouser mill was located.

Mister Clouser had a white picket fence surrounding his lot and his property which consisted of 192 acres. But along with their business and beautiful home, the family also had a mysterious ghost. Each Christmas Eve, the shadowy figure of a man dressed in Shawnee Indian garb would show up as a dark, ominous figure at the end of the path leading to their house. He would stand there, staring up at the house and just outside the little wooden yard fence. As the family peered fearfully through the windows, he would gesture desperately to them, using hand signals as if trying to communicate to the family. The Clousers would hover there stupefied with fear, too scared to move until the ghost faded away into the darkness.

Each year this would happen and the Clousers would wait in mortified anticipation, believing perhaps the Native Indian was cursing them because long ago, his people once freely roamed this very land they now owned. Time passed before they found out the truth. Much earlier, a Native Indian had been murdered on the lush mixture of woods and field near Fallsville. It was rumored he had been followed by thieves, but before he was killed, he buried his treasures somewhere near where the town of Fallsville would later stand. The Clousers came to believe the Shawnee was trying to tell them where his treasure was buried. Yet, they could never translate his hand signals, nor decipher his mouthed words that might reveal where his wealth was hidden.

All that remains intact of Fallsville is the historic Auburn Methodist Church of Fallsville (historical) The Clouser family plot is in front of the image.

It is said the ghost of the Native Indian still appears where the old homestead once stood. It is overgrown there now along the old gravel Falls Lane. The town is gone except a little white church and the graveyard where the Clousers are buried. The Clouser home is nothing more than a pile of old stones and posts.

The old Clouser property and the place where the Native Indian appeared.

However, you can still walk through the town of Fallsville – it is now within Fallsville Wildlife Area. You can see the beautiful Clear Creek with its waterfalls and the old homestead (a tangled pile of moss-covered foundation stones, a fallen picket fence, the old concrete walkway where the ghost stood and a well. There is also an old quarry). And perhaps any time of the year, if the time is right, you might see the Shawnee spirit, read his hand signs and discover the treasure hidden somewhere nearby.

This is Fallsville Wildlife area. Seasonally, it is used for hunting and you must follow Division of Wildlife regulations when visiting.

Leesburg Will-o'-wisps

Jack-o-lanterns and will-o'-wisps are ghostly lights that flicker much like the light within a lantern. Throughout the ages, it was believed that these glowing lights were used to draw curious travelers from the safety of the trails they were on and into some kind of mischief. The Highland Weekly News reported about these strange lights in 1885, warning those wandering the roadway outside Leesburg to be wary of trouble.

> *Someone is trying to start a ghost sensation or rather a "Jack-o lantern" story. A queer light has been seen along a low tract of land south of the railroad about a mile east of town, two or three times recently, and it is believed by those who saw it to be a "Jack-o lantern" or Will-o-wisp." At any rate it is not safe to hunt chickens in that region after dark.*
>
> ***The Highland Weekly News. (Hillsboro, Ohio) April 15, 1885.***

In days gone by, people used to swim in Scotts Creek just outside Logan, Ohio. Once in a while these days, you can see a car or two parked along the gravel pull-off near a sharp turn on State Route 93 where folks now stop to fish along the same creek bank.

It is terrifying that very few know there is a dangerous deep spot along the creek near the falls where the rock drops downward 15 or so feet, then juts upstream. It looks shallow, and it can be a death trap for anyone getting caught within.

But perhaps to some, there is something even more frightening there that even fewer may know. Two ghosts are known to stalk this very creek bed along with the horse team and wagon they road upon 127 years ago.

The newspapers called it an AWFUL CALAMITY. And it transpired in the deep summer of 1887 when newlyweds 29 year-old Johannes and 19 year-old Clara Bensonhafer were taking a load of wheat to the local mill in Logan.

They traveled along what is now a part of State Route 93 but was then called Scotts Creek Road. They paused to cross what they believed to be a shallow ford near Scotts Creek Falls. But it was not shallow there at all. The horses plunged forward, pulling the heavy load and those riding the wagon with them. Clara and Johannes were drowned immediately along with their horses. It was not until their hats and a basket were seen floating in the creek the call of alarm in Logan was given out.

Deadly Gulf. A Team and Two People Drowned, Near the Falls of Scott's Creek. The Sad Ending of the Lives of Mr. And Mrs. John Bensenhaver.

On Tuesday morning last a young couple, who, but a few months ago began married life together at the home of Mrs. Bensenhaver's mother who is Mrs. Silas Nixon, of near Ewing, this county, were in full life and health, and in a wagon loaded with wheat started from their home to Logan. When they arrived at the ford immediately above the falls of Scott's Creek, it is supposed they drove their team into the stream to allow their horses to drink, all unconscious of the fate that awaited them. . . ***The Ohio Democrat. (Logan, Ohio) August 20, 1887.***

The young couple were pulled too late from the water and their bodies buried in nearby Ewing Cemetery. But on some nights, it is said you can hear the grind of wagon wheels along the roadway followed by the muffled talk of the young couple as their ghostly wagon slips off State Route 93 and to the bank near the falls. Then there are the screams of horses as the phantom team descends into the murky, deep depths of Scotts Creek and disappear into the nothingness below.

These two images were taken in succession at Scott's Creek above the falls. If you look closely and below each arrow, you can see a woman on the left, a man in the center carrying another man over his shoulders and a team of horses on the right. From the first to the second image, they have moved closer to me and changed position.

The Old Man of Old Man's Cave

Legends have always been told of the ghost of the old man who would wander the valley area now known as Old Man's Cave. The cave is located about an hour drive from Columbus and a little more than a stone's throw from the Hocking Hills Visitor Center. Visitors for well over a hundred years have reported watching his apparition meander the well-worn trail along the small Cedar Valley Creek within the gorge. From there, he works his way upward to the recess cave where he vanishes at the place his body was found. As he walks, the old man always has his flintlock rifle propped lazily on his shoulder and a white hound saunters by his side.

In fact, a reporter for the Logan Democrat-Sentinel gave an account that occurred on a sunny, hot Sunday, August 11th 1907. A Mister Kreig and Mister Hillis were setting up a rope near Old Man's Cave about 150 feet above Cedar Valley Creek. Once set, they would descend the rope until they were about 50 feet above the waters of the creek below, then they would take turns swinging across the valley entertaining both themselves and the amused tourists visiting the cave.

Cliff over Lower Falls and Cedar Valley Creek where Kreig and Hillis were swinging on the rope. The old man was seen entering on the platform of rock left of waterfall.

The two men watched curiously as an elderly, and white-bearded man wearing strange old-fashioned clothing entered the cave from the western end. He had a rifle propped up on one shoulder and a peculiarly large dog walked by his side. As Mister Hillis carefully descended the rope to swing, the old man stopped to watch the antics seemingly as absorbed in the performance as the tourists milling around. Thereafter, he worked his way through the onlookers, pausing now and then with his dog to watch those touring the cave . . .

. . . He gazed with eager interest at Mr. Kreig while he was swinging across Cedar Valley Creek, some 50 feet above the waters. The old man then passed on east, where the two Misses Dickens and Messrs. Carpenter and Frampton of Logan, were gathering ferns and mosses, here he paused for about 15 or 20 minutes and watched these young people decorating themselves with spruce and wild flowers, with which the cave is infested. Now he passed on north a few rods where Lewis, Vern and George Conkle and Herbert Lovesey were amusing themselves by rolling rocks into Cedar Creek some 50 feet below. Here the old man walked up to the edge of the rocks and leaned over so that he could watch the rocks in their precipitation till they struck the water below. He then turned west again, and started back the same direction he came, only a little farther north. He had traveled only 20 or 25 rods when he came past where Mr. Frank Lindsey and Miss Cora Linn were seated on a rock engaged in pleasant conversation. The young lady not knowing of the strange visitor became frightened when she saw the old man with gray hair and long white beard standing in front of them, and fainted away, but by administering opiates she was revived. The old man looked at Miss Icel Davis with a smile, who was standing near about ready to get scared and run away, as if to say, I did not come here to frighten anyone, especially young ladies. He now went to the base of the rock near by, and looked into a cavern that was supposed to be the place where the old man and his dog slept. This place was legibly marked in English print. Near this place there seems to be a depression in the ground about two feet below the elevation of the cave. All eyes now seemed to be fixed on the old man and his dog to see where they would go next, what was their surprise when the old man and his dog, almost in the twinkling of an eye, sank down into the ground in the above named depression. . . ***The Democrat-sentinel., (Logan, Ohio) August 15, 1907***

Old Man's Cave—also referred to as "Dead Man's Cave."

There was a certain mystery as to where this old ghost originated. From the testimonies of those hailing from the town of Cedar Grove nearby, the old man was said to be discovered by two local boys exploring the cave in the 1800s. Growing bored after climbing upon the rocks one afternoon, they built a small fire within the recess. Moments later, the crunch of footsteps on leaves and sand forced them to look up from the flames of their newest project. An elderly man with a long, gray beard, wearing old -fashioned clothing and leather moccasins walked right past them . . .

. . .The old man and his dog passed the boys. The old man looked at the boys with a smile, but said nothing to them, and the dog looked straight ahead, and stayed close to his master. The boys were amazed at the strange actions of the old man and dog, and so kept a close watch after the mysterious man and dog. They walked around the cave looking every where and finally they came to a standstill at one place near the edge of the rocks. On these rocks were considerable writing concerning the old man and his dog, and not far from this place was considerable depression or a place lower than the rest of the ground around it. And to this place it seemed that the old man and his dog were particularly attracted . . . ***The Democrat-sentinel., (Logan, Ohio) March 28, 1907. Interesting Story of Old Man's Cave***

To their surprise, after the man paused to stare at a depression in the sandstone, he sank to the ground and completely vanished. Eagerly, the boys sought help from some local adults at Cedar Grove in investigating the place the old man had disappeared. With mattocks and shovels, a small crew of men removed rocks and dug out the hollow in the sandstone floor of the cave. . .

. . .We then removed the dirt and sand along this surface, when we found it to be a box or something of the kind. On the top, it was about 6 X 4 ft. On further examination we found this box to be some kind of earthen ware and of a porous nature so that the water could penetrate through it. We found a lid neatly fit on this box, as we may call it for want of a better name. We then ascertained that this lid was loose, and lifting the lid from the box, there was the old man and dog looking the same as the boys had represented them to us. The soil and water by which they were in and surrounded, had caused them to be in a state of petrifaction, and were as natural as they had appeared to the boys in their spiritual vision. And there they lay sleeping as it might seem as contently as two little brothers. . . ***The Democrat-sentinel., (Logan, Ohio) March 28, 1907. Interesting Story of Old Man's Cave***

The old man's name was given as 'Retzler', and the name of his dog was 'Harpor', and his gun 'Pointer', bearing the date -1702.

Upon further digging, the men were able to find cooking utensils and a flintlock rifle that had the date of 1702 engraved upon it. In an earthen pot, they found a paper in English print claiming that King George III had rights to tax the American colonies, a copy of the Declaration of Independence and a journal dating the old man's death as 1777.

. . . He came to the cave, which bore his name in 1750. He was a trapper. He and 25 other trappers came to this part of the country at the same time. He selecting this cave for his abode, and his companions locating in different places along Cedar Valley Creek, living in wigwams, and trapping, and that their furs were gathered up by agents at regular intervals, and that they all grew rich. It was also stated that the old man died in 1777 and was buried by his companions, and that his dog was alive in the coffin by the side of his master and buried. And also that his gun, property and wealth was near his grave. The next we found in the bottom of the vessel was gold coins to the amount of six or seven hundred dollars. . . ***The Democrat-sentinel., March 28, 1907. Interesting Story of Old Man's Cave***

From 1905 and well through 1909, there were numerous mentions of the ghost visiting the cave area where he would disappear in the depression of his grave.

It is reported that the Old man and his white dog make their appearance every day, it is alleged that the old man has been known to speak to passerbys, and that his dog has been heard barking in and around the cave. ***The Democrat-sentinel., February 25, 1909.***

Two of our boys were out coon hunting one night last week. After the boys had amused themselves for some time, they came around to Old Man's Cave. They claim that the old man and his dog met them at the entrance to the cave. The old man was very large the boys said and looked like he would weigh at least 300 pounds, he was oddly dressed and wore a large plug hat and hauled a flint lock gun on his shoulder. His dog was larger than our dogs of today and was white as snow. . . ***The Democrat-sentinel., December 17, 1908. Cedar Grove.***

And to this day, there are still reports of the old man roaming the cave with his dog and the low echo of a hound baying deep into the night. As far as the old man, just keep your eyes peeled during your visit to Old Man's Cave. You just might see him walking the trail before he disappears where he was once buried.

Old Warwick

During the 1800s, African Americans settled in Berlin Crossroads including Thomas Woodson, a former slave of President Thomas Jefferson. Many townspeople, including the Woodsons, opened their homes to runaway slaves on the Underground Railroad.

A Special Edition to the Cincinnati Enquirer on September 12th, 1894 reported that a terrific storm rumbled across southern Ohio the day before. In its wake, it destroyed an ancient stone mansion that was located in Berlin (Crossroads) near Jackson, Ohio. The mansion was known as being quite old and haunted even in that time. Originally built by Robert Warwick , the son of an English Lord, he ran out of funds to pay his workmen just as the structure was almost finished.

Undaunted, he took on the labor himself and toiled so hard at finishing the magnificent home, he became sick. The mansion fell to creditors and Robert Warwick, heartsick, died.

> *. . . The exertion proved too much. For months he lay sick, and the new mansion, the pride of his heart, finally passed into the hands of his creditors. The dying man never recovered from the loss. Just a few moments before his death he arose from his bed, and pacing about the rooms like a madman, he pronounced a horrible curse upon the building and upon those who should ever afterward make it their abode. For years after his death the neighbors refused to venture near the stately manor, and many claimed that they could see the ghost of "Old Warwick" appear in white at the windows at night. . . .*
> ***Cincinnati Enquirer (Cincinnati, Ohio) Author SPECIAL DISPATCH TO THE ENQUIRER Sep 12, 1894 page 1***

But just a few moments before he passed, the man arose from his bed and paced back and forth, cursing the home and anyone who would live in it. No one dared go near it and even when families moved into it, they met some horrible fate. By 1880, the house became abandoned. And then came the storm and the terrible fire. The newspaper title stated boldly: "Old Warwick Arose in the Seething Flames. And his oldtime wailing was again heard." Because within the walls as it burned that early September night, those who watched the fire dance along the walls heard the voice of Robert Warwick screaming curses into the air and his apparition vanishing into the flames of the fire with the mansion.

Fairmount Cemetery was established in 1867 and then called Union Cemetery. Before that, the Gay Street Cemetery was the main burying place for those who lived and died in Jackson, Ohio. It was located in an outlying section of Jackson County called "Jamestown." Apparently sometime after Fairmount was opened for burials, it had . . . a ghost!

> *The citizens of Jamestown are seeing a ghost. Not any of your airy nothings, but a regular out-and-out spook—one of the kind that it makes little boy's hair stand erect to tell about. This ghost dresses in white, and stalks about scaring people almost into spasms. It is said to be the spook of a well known citizen, now dead, and to come nightly from the new cemetery. We would mildly suggest to our Jimtown friends that no well regulated ghost can stand a load of bird shot without materializing on the spot. One load fired into the ghost will spoil that ghost story.*
> ***The Jackson standard., (Jackson, Oh)October 06, 1881. A Spook!***

Empire

Empire, Ohio 43926

The Illustrious Ghost of Nancy Weir

A street in McCoy's Station today.

Found Murdered.

Steubenville, O., June 9.—At McCoy's station near Steubenville, Mrs. Nancy Weir was found dead in her room with her throat cut from ear to ear and with several knife wounds on her body and on one hand. Near her body lay a penknife. It is supposed that the woman was murdered. Ed Householder, of McCoy's, has been arrested at Steubenville on suspicion of being the murderer. The Stark County Democrat., (Canton, Ohio) June 10, 1886. Found Murdered.

The two had been quarreling on Sunday night and into Monday early morning of June 7th, 1886 when this ghost story began. No neighbors recalled what they heard through the worn wooden walls of the boarding house room the two shared, but the woman was angry and the man was drunk.

32 year-old Edward Householder and his mistress, 38 year-old Mrs. Nancy (Mushrush) Weir, had gotten into a horrible, horrible fight. He left and at 6 o'clock the next evening, they found her dead.

Edward Householder was apprehended for the crime. He would plead his case, blaming the murder on bad women and whiskey. His defense may not have been completely flawed. There was an incident a little less than 20 years earlier involving the same Mrs. Weir perhaps aiding and abetting in a murder, herself. This murder happened on a Saturday evening, April 6th, 1867 when a prominent citizen in town, Lewis K. McCoy met Joseph McDonald at the train station and shot him with his carbine over an ongoing dispute. Murder. It was suggested Nancy Weir was having an affair with Mister McCoy at the time. And that she had a hand in the murder somehow.

This little ditty was brought to the attention of others in the newspaper:

> *Steubenville, O., June 7 [Special] 6 o'clock this evening Nancy Weir, a woman aged about 38 years, was found dead at McCoy's Station, this county, with her throat cut from ear to ear and several stabs on her breast. She had a penknife in her hand. It is not known whether it is a case of suicide or murder, but the general belief is that she was murdered and the knife afterward placed in her hand. The woman is well known from the fact that she was closely connected with the murder of McDonald some years ago at that place, having been mistress of Lewis K. McCoy, the murderer, who was sent to the penitentiary for life, after spending $ 100,000 in his defense.* ***Cleveland Plain Dealer Historical Archives (Cleveland, Ohio) June 8, 1886***

Nancy's Grave in Toronto Union Cemetery.

Regardless of Mrs. Weir's illustrious past, Edward's weak defense didn't sit too well with the judge. It didn't help Edward admitted that he didn't even remember killing Nancy. He had blood spatters on his shirt when apprehended. A certain knife belonging to Mister Edward Householder, covered with blood, was found lying near the dead Nancy Weir's body. A blue flannel shirt that witnesses attested Edward wore the day before her death, was found saturated with blood and hidden behind a trunk in the room. Unlike Lewis K. McCoy who was pardoned in 1870 and quietly lived out the rest of his life in town, Edward Householder was convicted of manslaughter and sentenced to 10 years in prison. Nancy Weir was buried in Toronto Union Cemetery just up the road.

***Edward Householder, the murderer of his mistress, Nancy Weir, at McCoys station, last June, was found guilty of manslaughter, last June, in Jefferson common pleas, and sentenced by Judge Hance to ten years' imprisonment in the penitentiary. The felon charges bad women and whisky with his downfall.* Belmont Chronicle., (St. Clairsville, Ohio) April 28, 1887.**

And all should have been said and done. But the souls of those tragically departed tend to rest not so easily. And so it was with the infamous Nancy Weir. It was not long after her death boarders living in the home she had been murdered complained of seeing her ghost. Their claims were disregarded with a roll of eyes. That is, until a stranger came to town who didn't know the story and saw her ghost.

His name was A. Ashbrook, a drummer by trade. *Drummer* being an old-fashioned term for traveling salesman —one time, these peddlers would bang a drum to get people's attention of their wares. He hadn't planned on stopping at McCoy's Station. He was just passing through on his way to New Cumberland just across the Ohio River. However, he could not cross the river because of the ice flowing heavily on this particular March day. Reluctantly, he decided to spend the night in McCoy's Station because it was getting so late.

Yet, the hotel was filled and the only place left to stay was a boarding house in town. Mister Ashbrook was assigned his room there and prepared himself for bed. . .

> *Upon retiring he left the lamp burning and, being tired, was soon in slumber. Today he told his experience: He says a dread feeling came over him about midnight, as though some other person was in the room. He opened his eyes and looking in the direction of the lamp saw sitting on a chair a rather attractive woman, wearing a man's white hat and clad in a brown calico dress. Ashbrook asked what was wanted, but received no reply. He then arose and approached the woman and when about to lay his hand upon her the apparition vanished and the lamp was blown out. Thinking that he had had a bad case of nightmare Ashbrook retired again. This morning he related the facts as told. The singular feature of the case is that Mr. Ashbrook was not acquainted with the murder and his description is almost perfect as to the looks and manner of dress of Nancy Weir when she was killed a year ago. Plain Dealer [Cleveland, Oh] 10 March, 1888: p. 1 JEFFERSON COUNTY. A Drummers Yarn.*

She came to him that night, slipping into the room. Nancy Weir's ghost sat by a lamp, clothed in a brown calico dress and a man's white hat. And when he arose and reached out a hand to touch her, she completely vanished into the air. Dead, she may have been, but the illustrious ghost of Nancy Weir would stick around for many years to let others know she was there.

Camp Sychar

201 Sychar Road
Mt Vernon, Ohio 43050
40.406653, -82.469140

He Guards the Spring

Entrance Camp Sychar—1911. Courtesy: The Denzer Collection Knox Times.

In the 19th century a holiness movement began and religious camp meetings were held across the United States by a multitude of different churches, including the Methodist Church. One, The Ohio State Camp Meeting Association held camp meetings in different cities until transporting the tents from town to town became a hardship. Undeterred, they settled on a rural area about 2 miles outside the city proper of Mt. Vernon and built a campground and accommodations for people to stay during the meetings. Because of the fresh spring that came from within the camp, they named it Camp Sychar for a deep well in the bible denoted by the name "Well of Sychar."

Camp Sychar campground.

Courtesy: The Denzer Collection Knox Times.

Fountain/pump from spring in foreground.
Courtesy: The Denzer Collection Knox Times.

In fact, the pure spring water was so good at this new camp outside Mt. Vernon, they wanted to share it with the community. A pipe was laid to a trough about 50 feet away and along the main roadside outside this little camping village. People would come from miles around to drink the fresh, cool water from Camp Sychar.

It wasn't long before the land around it became of use, too. A park was built across the roadway and Christian-based school, called Academia, was erected on the property. A railway was even added to connect the village, camp and park. But it wasn't long after the camp was dedicated strange stories began popping up about a peculiar apparition seen moving about the spring.

Those who saw it all described this ghostly form the same as printed in the November 21st, 1897 Cincinnati Enquirer:

> *It was always described as being tall, gaunt, and clad in the attire of a minister. Under his arm he INVARIABLY CARRIED A BOOK. Which was readily supposed to be the Bible. In all the positions in which he has ever been seen he was always described as guarding the spring, as though it were sacred and under divine direction.* ***Cincinnati Enquirer***

It was right around 1892 when the first rumors began to arise about the ghost. A groundskeeper on the Camp Sychar property insisted he saw a tall, gaunt man dressed as a minister near the spring. So disturbed was he by the ghost, he quit his job. Many times over the years, the railroad workers coming down the tracks late at night, too, saw the ghostly apparition appear and disappear. Most of the time, they kept these sightings to themselves.

It was not until the autumn of 1897 when a sighting left two men so troubled, they contacted local newspapers to tell their story:

> *Several weeks ago a traveling man named Balfour and a companion, having the night to spend in the city, boarded the cars and went out to the park to while away a few hours before retiring for the night. The regular season at the park closed in September after which time cars ceased to run after 9 o'clock at night. The gentlemen were not aware of this fact, and, after alighting at the entrance, sauntered up into the grounds and did not think of returning until long after the cars had stopped for the night. When they arrived at the entrance they found*
>
> *EVERYTHING IN DARKNESS.*
>
> *And after waiting until they were convinced that they would be compelled to walk to the city, set out for their return. Being unacquainted with the country they failed to take the regular roadway, but tramped in along the tracks, a much longer and tiresome route. . .*

Pathway where ghost was seen. Courtesy: The Denzer Collection Knox Times.

By the time they had reached Sychar they were thirsty and noticing as they went out that a spring emptied into a trough at the roadside, they turned in to get a drink. They were tired and tramped along in silence. When they had reached the trough Balfour looked over the fence. His heart almost stopped at the sight that met his gaze. Speechlessly he nudged his companion and pointed. There before them was the ghostly sentinel pacing to and fro in front of the spring. Both men stood and looked, being too much taken by surprise to speak. Plainly they could see the figure pace noiselessly back and forth and each time they could see the iron railing surrounding the spring shining through its body. Whenever they looked intently the shadow instantly cleared to an outline, and objects beyond it could be seen as clearly as through murky glass. They stood silently for several minutes watching the weird scene until one of them recovered sufficiently to speak, when the figure vanished like a fog before a midday sun. Returning to the city they told their story substantially as given above. Many theories are now advanced for the appearance of this specter at so unusual a place. One is that long ago an old hermit lived near the spring and that it was his ghost that has returned to guard the waters. Another is that among the party of Methodists who sought this spot for their meeting grounds was an old minister who was particularly moved in his choice on account of the spring, and that it is his spirit that stands such zealous guard over the spring. ***Cincinnati Enquirer, Special Dispatch to the Enquirer. November 21, 1897 Page 17. Strange Apparition of a Man That Guards the Spring at Camp Sychar***

It wouldn't seem so surprising a spirit would decide to stick around Camp Sychar, especially if it is a bible-toting minister and one that has touched so many lives over time. For well over 140 years, the events at the camp have boosted the souls of thousands of church-goers. It has provided a spiritual retreat. Perhaps Camp Sychar's spring-side ghost knows there is just one more person stopping in for a refreshing drink whose soul just might be saved.

The cement roadside spring outside the picturesque Camp Sychar is in the forefront. When this picture was taken, it was used as a planter.

Licking County Jail

Inmates of the Licking County Jail still haunt the building. The sound of rattling shackles echo through hallways, voices are heard and strange images show up on photographs. People also attest to seeing full-body apparitions.

Built in 1889, it has housed serial killers, murderers and even the insane. There were at least 18 deaths within those walls, seven of those being suicides. Four of the deaths were sheriffs who died from heart attacks. In 1910 a Dry Agent Detective for the Anti-saloon League, 17 year-old Carl Etherington, was visiting the city of Newark, arresting saloon owners illegally selling alcohol. After a scuffle with the local police where an officer was killed, he was placed in jail. There, he was beaten by a mob, dragged outside and then hanged in town while thousands watched. Now people see ghosts. You can see them too. Eric Glosser, a retired Newark police officer, manages the Licking County Jail. Ghost tours are offered. You can find information at: www.parajail.com.

Cottesbrook Farm Curve and Bridge over Black River

868-996 Oberlin Elyria Road
Elyria, Ohio 44035
41.336889,-82.120745

Lorain County

Elyria Trolley Ghost

Below: Lake Shore Electric Interurban car. Courtesy: The Cleveland Press Collection

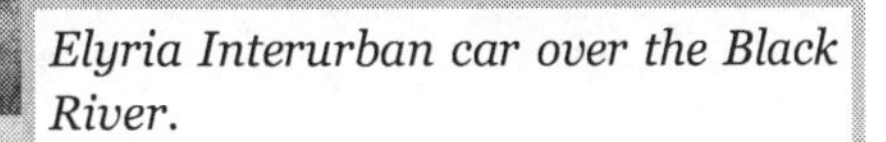

Elyria Interurban car over the Black River.

It was a hot summer evening in 1903, 6:30 on Sunday the 16th of July, to be exact. An electrically powered interurban railroad train trolley was making its way along the track about two miles southwest of Elyria. Just about the time it reached the Black River Bridge and a sharp veer called the Cottesbrook Curve, it came head-on into another interurban car. A misunderstanding of orders left both an eastbound and a westbound train on the same track. The two trains collided.

One of the most disastrous wrecks that has occurred in the vicinity of Elyria for years occurred at about 6:30 o'clock Sunday evening, just west of the bridge on the C. & S. W., near the Cottesbroke farm. E.L. Garvin, a well known printer of Oberlin, a former employee of The Chronicle office, was instantly killed, his neck being broken and his legs badly crushed. . . Car No. 99 which had only been out of the shop two or three days, was coming from Oberlin in charge of Conductor Mack and Motorman O'Brian with orders to meet two cars at the "Lowry" switch just east of the bridge. Car No. 67 in charge of Conductor Leonard and Motorman Murray, one of the old cars, with an express room in front which had been due to leave Elyria at 5:30 but was over half an hour late closely followed . . .At any rate, No. 67 passed the "Lowrey" switch, and was just at the bridge when No. 99 was seen rounding the curve too late to avoid a collision. Motorman Frank Murray of No. 67 escaped by jumping, No. 99 being one of the new heavy cars plowed into the older and lighter car, telescoping nearly half its length. . . ***The Elyria Chronicle, Elyria, Ohio Monday July 20, 1903. Electric Car Telescoped. Fatal Collision at the Black River Bridge in Carlisle.***

The ghost stories began to surface in December of that year. A trolley driver nearing the Cottesbroke Curve saw a shadowy figure standing still on the tracks in his path. He blew his whistle to warn the person standing there and slowed until he was nearly at a standstill. Just as the headlights fell where the shadowy figure had been, it completely vanished. Over the course of the month, this same shadowy form blocked his path on the tracks in front of his trolley in the exact same place.

In late December, two men were sent out to clear the tracks of snow at the Cottesbroke Curve. While sweeping the snow away, they heard the sounds of a trolley car approaching them . . .there was an explosion like that of two trolley cars meeting head-on and then, suddenly, silence. . .

Cottesbrooke curve

Both stepped back from the track to await the passing of the car. They could hear it approach. Nearer and nearer it came they claim, until its deafening noise was upon them, but no car was to be seen. No headlight broke the gloom of the whirling snow and no car flashed by them with its windows alight, they said.

Not a thing came out of the snow ahead of them, but the noise of rapidly moving car was plainly heard rushing by them, they said, until with a terrible crash, like the meeting of two cars, the noise of the onrushing car ceased.

A cry, of a human being in mortal anguish, followed the crash, they averred, then all was still as death. Standing for a second petrified with fear, the men gazed at one another, dropped their brooms, and in headlong flight stumbled over the tracks to the powerhouse.

Arriving there in the safety of the lighted powerhouse, with eager men crowding around them, the two section men, between gasps of horror, as the awful cry reverberated in their ears, told their story. They were laughed at and ordered to return to their work. But neither laughter nor threats could induce them to go back to the curve.

Their terrified glances behind them and the horror that looked from their startling eyes finally broke down the scoffing of their comrades, and when the motorman, who has previously been the only one to whom the apparition had appeared, maintained the truth of the ghostly invasion of Cottesbrooke curve, consternation seized upon the mind of the trolley men.

*Although some few still scoff, the majority of the men on the division dread the spot, and the night crews past the curve with bated breath and swelling heart, fearful of another visitation of the terrible apparition. **Wooster Weekly Republican. (Wooster, Ohio) January 27, 1904. Pg 5. Ghost Story***

Cottesbrooke curve where a ghost was seen by interurban drivers.

Now the place where the Cottesbrooke Curve was located is a busy intersection in town. Few people, if any, driving across the bridge could recount the accident that killed Edwin Garvin that July nightfall of 1903. Maybe the shadowy form they see where the old trolley used to travel appears nothing more than someone walking home late at night. And if they stop, perhaps like the trolley men before them, they simply rub their tired eyes and think it was nothing more than their imagination. But it isn't.

Barefoot Ghost on the Old Cherry Street Bridge—Toledo

It is known as the Martin Luther King Bridge now. It spans the Maumee River in Toledo, connecting Cherry Street with Main. But long ago when it was a different bridge and one that charged a toll to cross the river, it was known as the Cherry Street Bridge. Back then and when the first Cherry Street bridge was built in 1865, it was made of wood. It cost 2 cents a person to cross the bridge and a dime for a horse.

But between 1865 and 1883, the bridge would be wiped out by floods two times. Finally in 1884, a new steel bridge was built that would last until 1908. It was safe from floods, finally, but not being hit by steamships. In 1908 a boat hit the Cherry Street Bridge and a new concrete arch bridge was completed in 1914 to replace it.

The old haunted Cherry Street Bridge circa 1907.

Yet. if we take a step back in time to August of 1882 when the bridge was still made of wood and the new steel bridge of 1884 had yet to be built, there appeared a ghost there. It was not just one time, but countless times over the years, for many people crossed over to use this central business district and a busy section of town. A local shoemaker fondly called Pop Meyer had hanged himself there with a piece of rope, and soon after, so did his son . . . with the same rope.

Suicide at Toledo

SPECIAL DISPATCH TO THE ENQUIRER. TOLEDO, OHIO, *November 18.-Joseph Myers, aged about twenty-seven, and unmarried came home from a protracted spree at two o'clock this morning, and soon after that committed suicide by hanging himself in the yard, where he was found at daylight. He was the son of Joseph Myers, who hung himself on the Cherry-street Bridge last August and on this occasion he used the same rope with which his father had hung himself, and which he had kept in his trunk, evidently with some such purpose in view. Dissipation and probably remorse at the thought that he had helped bring about his father's death by his profligacy seemed to be the reason of his action.* ***Cincinnati Enquirer. (Cincinnati, Ohio) Nov 14, 1881. Suicide at Toledo. pg. 1***

Martin Luther King Bridge (AKA Cherry Street Bridge) in 2015.

In an interview with Detective Louis Trotter of the Toledo Police Department, a Cincinnati Enquirer reporter wrote this article in December of 1884—

Trotter tells the story like this:

Some of the boys who live on the East Side were going home from duty one August morning in 1882. When we reached the first pier I was horrified to see the body of someone hanging there. It did not take us long to cut the corpse down and we found it was Pop Meyers, as he was familiarly called. His face was just as pleasant as if he were selling a pair of shoes to a customer.

There was not the least sign of pain, and his wide-open eyes were looking rather expectantly up the river. He had evidently put on a new shirt, collar, and necktie, and was well dressed, except that he had no coat or shoes on. Well, we carried him home and found some letters which plainly indicated that his mind had left his body. His son, who had brought so much care on the old man's mind by his dissipation, begged us to give him the rope with which his father had hanged himself. 'I want it as a reminder,' he said, 'of my father.' Well, some way he obtained the rope, and with it, shortly afterward, ended his life at the identical spot, with the same rope. ***Special Dispatch to the Enquirer. (Cincinnati, Ohio) December 28, 1884. p. 13***

But soon after the deaths of the father and son, people began reporting a ghost on the bridge. The apparition was of a nicely dressed man dragging a rope. As he quietly plodded across the bridge, no sound was made. His feet were bare just as the police officers had found him when he hanged himself. In fact, Trotter went on to state:

> *"I investigated the affair and found it was true something was haunting the bridge. The ghost was dressed just as Meyer was on the morning that I cut him down. The old bridge was carried away, and the story was forgotten. The first night the new bridge was opened late wayfarers were badly frightened by a phantom walking slowly along in his bare feet, making no noise as he softly trod the planks. That's all I know about it. Officer Kruse states that many people have recently told him they had seen Meyers' ghost patrolling the bridge, rope in hand, after midnight."* ***Cincinnati Enquirer. (Cincinnati, Ohio). December 28, 1884. p. 13***

Even after the new bridge was built in 1884, the ghostly apparition of Meyer was seen on the bridge. It does not seem to deter the old ghost, that new bridges with new names have come after. There are still those out there who see a misty apparition walking along the Cherry Street Bridge when they cross over on foggy nights after midnight. And as long as people need to cross the Maumee, there probably always will!

Defunct Cemetery and Orchard

Plain City, Ohio 43064

Nora

Sometimes the ghostly places found in old legends are long gone. But the story is still interesting and worth the retelling. Such is the case of this old cemetery and orchard once found a bit outside Plain City, Ohio and the ghost of a girl named Nora who once haunted it.

In 1815, a building for the Lower Liberty Presbyterian Church was built on land outside Plain City . A cemetery soon followed. But the church eventually grew old and was abandoned. The bricks were dragged off to build a new Presbyterian Church.

The tiny graveyard filled with weeds and the stones began to decay. A few who moved into the neighborhood might add a grave or two. But by the time the Civil War came around, few even knew the church and cemetery had once been there.

Settlers would build on the land and not long after the church became extinct, a farmer and spiritualist set up home there with his wife and children around 1862. Among those living with the family was a young servant girl who most remembered only as Nora. She was rather pretty and was quite attracted to the farmer's son. It was certainly frowned upon in those times for the son of an employer to court a domestic. It was no different with these two. Perhaps the young man was not so much in love with the young woman or maybe the farmer forbade him to see her. Regardless, things turned out badly for poor Nora. Her cold body was found one morning hanging in a plum tree in the small farmyard orchard near the home. And she was buried in the ancient cemetery among the old church-goers and homesteaders like the Donalsons and the Ewings and many more whose names were lost to time. Then, not long after, the ghost of the dead girl began to be seen among those same thickets, near the roadway and around the old cemetery that was covered in tall grasses by then.

. . . On the same farm, and near the haunted thicket, now stands the neat farm dwelling of Mr. Harlan P. Wood, the scene of the present excitement. For several nights past he has attributed the throwing of stones through his window to a man whom he some time ago discharged from his service. But the man could not be found, and all of last night and to-day, at short intervals, stones and brickbats have been flying through the sitting room window, sometimes being thrown outward, by unseen hands. . . ***Fort Worth Daily Gazette. (Fort Worth, Texas). March 29, 1887 Lively Ghost***

This spirit was a quiet form, did not seem to bother anyone. Her name would probably be forgotten if not after some time, Harlan Wood and his family moved to the land. It was reported that cloverseed was thrown around the house and potatoes kept in a cellar bin would be found upstairs in a sitting room in a pile placed upon the floor. And even more compelling was that a local constable by the name of Donohoe came to the home to investigate. He crept to the cellar to keep an eye on the potatoes, perhaps discover who was taking them and placing them in the other room. Suddenly, he was grabbed by unseen hands, bound hand and foot and his eyes and mouth stuffed with cloverseed!

The story faded away in the newspapers. Whether the Wood family was bothered by those unseen, but lively, hands thereafter is not known. And if Nora's ghost still haunts the area around Plain City, she must have quieted down. Maybe her shadow simply blends into the horizon or she has vanished away like the old orchard and cemetery she used to haunt.

Hazelton and Struthers, Ohio

Train Tracks

Rough Life of the Rail Man

Struthers, Ohio. Photo Courtesy Columbus Metro Library. Photo by Schall

If life working the rails wasn't difficult enough, workers along the railway tracks between Hazelton and Struthers had to contend with aggressive ghosts—

> ***HAUNTED TRACKS. A Ghost Driving Railroad Employes Out of the Country. SPECIAL DISPATCH TO THE ENQUIRER.***
>
> *Youngtown, Ohio. October 13. Railroad men employed between Hazelton and Struthers claim that the track is haunted by a muscular ghost that has terrorized them and a number have resigned and sought employment elsewhere. An employee named Van Horn was attacked by the ghostly apparition and beaten until large welts were placed on his body and when he reached Struthers, fell exhausted. Several persons have been killed near the lonely place by trains and it is probable some practical jokers are working the ghost business but they have been unable to catch him or bring him down with revolvers.*
>
> ***Cincinnati Enquirer (Cincinnati, Ohio). Oct 14, 1891 page 9***

One-legged Shoestring Peddler

An April 1909 report came from the Cleveland Plain Dealer: SEE ONE-LEGGED GHOST. It appears prisoners confined at the Marion Jail were seeing the ghost of a one-legged shoestring peddler, nicknamed "Shoestring Jack", who had committed suicide in cell 1 only six months earlier. He had hung himself to death by tying a pair of his shoestrings around his neck. The sleeping quarters for the city firemen who were on duty were located just above the jail. Ira Shrock, a local fireman, complained often that he was awakened at night by the crunch of the dead shoestring peddler's wooden leg dragging across the gritty cement floor. *Crunch. Drag. Crunch. Drag. Crunch.* Not far behind, came the ghostly apparition of the shoestring peddler himself. The fireman did not sleep well. The Old City Hall & Fire Department building was on the corner of South Prospect and W Church Streets in Marion. It isn't there anymore. A parking lot has taken its place. Still, it should be pondered, if those using the parking there at night still hear the crunch and drag of that old peg leg of Shoestring Jack's. Or perhaps if you've parked there, you won't anymore.

Legend of Lottie Bader

Sometimes old ghost stories leave us with more mystery than fear. Digging deeply into the legend and attempting to dig up historical evidence to back it up isn't always easy. In the 1800s when many of these ghostly legends were perpetuated, word of mouth was the only way they were passed on. Such, those tales become a bit twisted by time and warped in the verbal passing from one person to the next.

Perhaps this mystery is what adds to the part that makes us shiver with fear. . . just like the Legend of Lottie Bader.

A local story in Medina County centers around a young spiritualist by the name of Charlotte Bader who held séances in her family's Sharon Township home. Charlotte, who was nicknamed *Lottie*, became sick with consumption and eventually died. But on the evening she passed, she asked her mother to prepare her some tea and toast. "And by the way, mother," Lottie added. "I wish to be buried near the door of our home so I can visit with you once in a while after I die."

Her last wishes were granted. Lottie was buried by the back door of the Bader homestead. Over the years, Lottie's mother made the dead woman tea and toast and set it upon the kitchen table in the evening before bed. The next morning, the teacup would be empty and the plate was left with nothing but crumbs.

After some time, Lottie Bader's body was moved to the Sharon Township Cemetery. Until the old Bader homestead she lived in was torn down, it was remarked upon that the building was truly haunted. So is the story true? It has been told that there is a grave in the Sharon Township Cemetery marked: Charlotte B. Died July 24th, 1858. Aged 25 years. We checked it out. Actually the grave states: Charlotte B. Wife of Orlando P. Brockway Died July 24th, 1858. Aged 25 years. As far as the Bader home? There is a tiny dot on the Medina County 1857 map that appears to show land owned by the Bader family.

So . . . sometimes you've got to make a choice. Stick with the old legend and get the shiver. Or have fun searching for the mysterious treasure leading to a ghost story. And so it is with the Ghost of Lottie Bader. We may never know if it is true or not, but it is still great to tell. And maybe try to dig up some morsel of the true and scary behind it.

Confederate Ghosts of Johnson's Island

Officers' Quarters.

Johnson's Island Circa early 1900s. From the Walter Havighurst Special Collections, Miami University Libraries, Oxford, Ohio.

Powder and Block House.

Johnson's Island is a small island located in northern Ohio's Sandusky Bay. In 1861, the U.S. Army leased 40 acres of land belonging to the island's owner, Leonard Johnson, to build a prison camp for Confederate soldiers during the Civil War.

Then, from 1862 to 1865, Confederate soldiers were kept there in a prison. The camp had a hospital, barracks, kitchen, dining area and cemetery for the prisoners. Disease and harsh winters took their toll on many of the soldiers. Nearly 200 died and are buried on the island.

Johnson's Island Confederate Soldiers Cemetery today. Center: the statue that Italian workers reported came alive while ghostly soldiers marched by.

The island later became a resort in the late 1800s. It was even quarried for limestone in the early 1900s. Then, a village was built for the 150 or so workers which included a general store, school, tavern and post office. The workers, who were 80% Italian, related many ghost stories over the years. According to a New York Times article in August of 2000, old legends were told that one stormy night in 1915, some of these Italian laborers working in the limestone and stone quarry on the island saw the Confederate statue at the cemetery turn from where it faced the lake, so that it was looking toward the graves behind it. Then, when it lifted its bugle high and blew a tune, ghostly soldiers in rotting Confederate uniforms slipped from the mist coming from the lake and marched away. Old-timers tell that quarry workers heard a constant humming of the song "Dixie" echoing across the old camp.

Vintage Ghost in the Clock Tower

It is nice once in a while to dig out old ghost stories from the not-too-distant past. Like vintage clothing, they can be taken out, tried on, worn again, and remembered. One such ghost story comes from an article in Cleveland's Sunday Plain Dealer in 1978. It mentions a ghostly apparition in the clock tower of the grand Perry County Courthouse in New Lexington.

The ghost would appear in the building (built in 1887) near dawn dressed in white. More than 19 people witnessed the ghostly figure and the police investigated the scene. Whether the vintage spirit has been seen trying on his ghostly attire at the tower in recent years is uncertain. But there are those who may remember him or her none-the-less.

Gregg-Crites Octagon House

Crites Road

Circleville, Ohio 43113

39.585556, -82.941944

Pickaway County

The Mystical Octagon House

Some people believe the Gregg-Crites Octagon House in Circleville is haunted. It is certainly a unique site a stone's throw from a small subdivision and settled into a corn field not far from the Wal-Mart Supercenter property where it originally stood before the retail outlet moved in.

The house is nearly 160 years old and looks every bit its age right now. The paint is peeling and the doors and windows are covered with insulation board. But for some reason, it doesn't look lonely sitting there. Maybe it knows the Roundtown Conservancy is working on getting it spruced up a bit for future children's learning activities (and adult architectural classes).

Besides, outside its walls and a bit down the road, Wal-Mart and McDonalds and a dozen or so other stores and restaurants are doing a bustling business. The Circleville pumpkin water tower lays on its horizon. And within its walls, a few ghosts keep the dust company. In fact, Vanessa Boysel, a professional Psychic Medium and owner of Mystical Gardens just down the road, who offers tours there says people hear voices inside. They have been punched, pushed and had their hair pulled. The smell of coffee or ham and beans long gone have wafted in the air and both shadows and figures have startled folks.

13 Ghostly Taps at Brubaker Covered Bridge

Brubaker Covered Bridge passes over Sandy Run near the small Ohio town of Gratis. The legend centering around its ghostly past, as farfetched as it might seem, provides a vivid explanation for the curious events occurring for those who stop at the bridge: Back in the 1930s, a carload of teens was heading back from a grange dance in town. The car was going at a high rate of speed around a turn on the slender Brubaker Road when it hit the bridge head on. Everyone in the car was tossed out, dead at the scene.

The accident wasn't discovered until the next morning when a nearby farmer passed through the bridge and saw the carnage within. Twelve bodies were pulled from the creek bed of Sandy Run and the roadway that tragic day. Strangely, though, witnesses at the dance claimed to have seen 13 teens get into the car the night before.

Perhaps they were right. It wasn't long after the wreck, cars going through the bridge would stall unexpectedly. A dull but carefully spaced tap-tap-tap would be heard 13 times on the windshield before a whimpering "shhhh" swept up from Sandy Run and filtered through the windows like the gasp of a last dying breath. Many held on to the belief there were actually 13 people in the car and one body was never found, pulled downstream and lost. In fact, still today, those going through the bridge have experienced the stalling, the taps and then the whispering "shhh" as if the 13th victim is still trying to get the attention of those within to find him.

White Shades of Death at Bell Cemetery

Bell Cemetery is a small graveyard tucked within the farmland outside Eaton. It is a private cemetery and a locked fence keeps it safe from vandals. However, you do not need to go inside to see ghosts. Accounts of strange white objects floating around the cemetery have been reported from drivers along East Lexington Road.

What Little Turtle Left Behind

Fort St. Clair in Eaton is haunted by the ghosts of soldiers who were killed during a battle there.

The land making up Preble County was once considered a neutral ground among the native Indians—Miamis, Wyandots, Delawares, Mingoes and Shawnee —who used the mix of meadow and woodland abundant with wildlife mainly as a hunting ground. However, as the whites began to settle the region, fighting would break out in the small towns and communities between Native Indians and the early pioneers.

Fort Saint Clair in Eaton was built in 1792 to protect area settlers against these attacks of Native Indians. It was a little over a few acres and contained the basics of most early stockades including block houses and officer quarters.

Little Turtle, also known as *Meshekenoghqua,* was a chief of the Miamis at this time who lived along the Little and Great Miami Rivers in Southern Ohio and also the Maumee River in northern Ohio. On November 6th of 1792, Little Turtle led 250 Mingo and Wyandot Indians against 100 Kentucky riflemen camping just outside Fort Saint Clair. Six of the riflemen died and Little Turtle would go down in history as the key figure in defeating the army there. Other skirmishes would ensue, but Little Turtle and those he led were eventually pushed back and away from Preble County.

Now the old fort and battlefield are a part of the city of Eaton park system. Within, there is a large oak tree near the graveyard where the six soldiers were buried. Deemed the Whispering Oak, it has a story to tell. Legends say that if you sit quietly beneath it and listen to the rustle of the leaves, you can hear the story of the events the soldiers went through during the battle on that November day of 1792.

The spectral scent of camp smoke has been known to linger in the air even when no fires are burning nearby. And the ghostly apparition of a Kentucky rifleman slips along the carefully mown grass where the fort once stood.

Curse of Devil's Backbone

The Devil's Backbone along Old State Route 725 and Paint Creek has a legend dating back to the 1700s.

Devil's Backbone is a gorge on private land running along Paint Creek just outside Camden, Ohio. There is an old legend centered on this section of land that was also known as Backbone Hill. Hundreds of years ago, the bones and tools of Miami Indians were laid to rest on this hill by their families. It was a sacred place and one meant to remain undisturbed.

And so it would endure as a place of rest long into the 1700s and until General Anthony Wayne defeated the Miamis and other Ohio Indians at the Battle of Fallen Timbers in Northern Ohio in 1794. With the signing of the Treaty of Greenville, the Miamis surrendered their lands.

Devil's Backbone. Young campers at Camp Cartwright, once located near the 'Backbone', may remember hiking along the old road and hearing the ghostly tales of a murdered man haunting the land and the legend of Red Turtle's curse.

A Miami Indian chief by the name of Red Turtle was one of many Native Indians forced to relinquish the lands of Ohio in the late 1790s through the early 1800s, and such he had to leave his relatives buried on Devil's Backbone. He warned the white men who would live there that the ghosts of Indian warriors would remain to guard those graves. If any were disturbed, they could expect a quick retribution.

His curse was not taken lightly and the fear of the curse still remains today. Perhaps it is behind a cupped palm and a soft whisper to another ear, but some community members have long blamed an unusually high number of accidents and mishaps around the town of Camden on Red Turtle's curse.

One such incident was that of Franklin Bourne, a wealthy farmer and engineer, living just along the Devil's Backbone in the early 1900s. He simply vanished near Easter in 1912. Whispers began to slip through the town that he had been digging a garden in his yard and had accidently dug up some bones. Bones, many believed, to be that of Red Turtle's people. Gone, he was and a farmhand working for him insisted Bourne had left town and asked him to sell off his property and send him the money. The ruse lasted until Bourne's unrecognizable, decomposing body was found wrapped in a blanket and buried in a shallow grave 3 feet deep in his garden on June 10th of the following year after family members insisted the grounds be thoroughly searched.

FARMHAND ARRESTED *Rich Farmer Who Disappeared a Year Ago, Believed Murdered. Eaton, O., June 2, Elwood Davis, 40, a farmhand and single, is under arrest, suspected of having killed his employer.*

Davis' alleged victim Is Frank Bourne, 60, who owned a farm valued at $12,000 near Camden, in this, Preble county. Davis worked for him. Bourne disappeared a year ago and since then nothing authentic has been heard from him. His body had not been found, and, suspecting Davis to have killed his relative, John E. Bourne, a cousin, living in Middletown—swore out an affidavit, charging Davis with first degree murder. Davis was arrested soon afterward by Sheriff Werts.

Some time after his mysterious disappearance, Davis is said to have received a strange letter telling him to sell Bourne's effects and send the proceeds south, as Bourne intended to make his future home there. The sale was made. Neighbors say Davis had plenty of money to spend. ***The Democratic Banner., June 03, 1913. (Mt Vernon, Ohio). Farmhand Arrested.***

Elwood Davis was found guilty of the murder and sent to the Ohio State Penitentiary where he died in 1936. He had hit Bourne in the back of the head with an axe, stole his money. But rumors would persist that Red Turtle's curse had something to do with the man's death. And Franklin Bourne is rumored to still walk his land.

Hopewell Cemetery Bobbing Light

The Hopewell Associate Reformed Church and Cemetery began their existence with little more than a rough log building on the property in 1808. It was built by Scotch-Irish settlers who had left the south because of their strong belief against slavery. By 1826, the building was replaced with the one present today.

The cemetery nearby was the first public graveyard in Israel Township and the earliest known burial was in 1813. The cemetery is still active . . . and not just for new burials. A bobbing light has been seen roaming through the graves much like the flicker of a lantern.

Lida Griswold –Ghostly Librarian

The original Eaton Public Library as it appeared when Lida Griswold worked there. Courtesy: Columbus Metropolitan Library.

Mrs. Lida Griswold was the first permanent librarian for the Eaton Library. Her duties began in 1901 and ran until 1909 when she was brutally murdered by Harry Rife—

On July 8th, 1909, Lida Griswold was alone in the library with her 13 year-old son, Cloyd, and her sister. There was but one patron left in the room, a gentleman who had slipped quietly into the library and was now reading a book.

As it was closing time. Missus Griswold arose and made the customary announcement that the library was closing and all patrons must leave. To her horror, the man stood and began walking toward her with a gun in his hand.

He declared he would end it all, shot her and then turned the gun on himself. If she called out his name, the newspapers never stated. But Missus Griswold would have known him only as a suitor she had rejected. Missus Griswold was killed. She was buried in the local graveyard, Mound Cemetery. Her perpetrator, a married man by the name of Henry Rife, only grazed his own skin. He would be executed for his crime in 1910.

KILLS PUBLIC LIBRARIAN.

Eaton, July 9. –Henry Rife, a lineman, shot and killed the public librarian, Mrs. Lida Griswold, 38, in the public library here. Rife then attempted suicide. He sustained but a slight wound and was locked up in jail. The slain librarian was a daughter of Judge J.A. Gilmore. The tragedy was witnessed by the 12-year-old son of Mrs. Griswold. Rife, who has a wife and children is alleged to have been paying attention to the woman he killed and it is thought resentment led to the killing. ***The Evening Telegram. (Elyria, Ohio) July 9, 1909. KILLS PUBLIC LIBRARIAN.***

Lida's grave (front) at the Gilmore family plot in section 13. Mists have been reported near the grave.

The Eaton Public Library today.

Lida Griswold was an integral part of the library's founding and for this, she took her job as librarian quite seriously. Perhaps it is this and the love for her work that brings her spirit back to Eaton Public Library once in a while for a visit. Although a new building replaced the one where she was murdered, she makes herself known at the library once in a while.

Preble County Courthouse

101 E Main Street #203
Eaton, Ohio 45320
39.743626,-84.635864

Haunted Courthouse

The Preble County Courthouse was dedicated in 1918 on ground that had been used for the county courthouses since the mid-1800s. It shouldn't be surprising, then, that staff have claimed to hear doors opening on the second floor. Footsteps are heard throughout the building and the front door has rattled when locked as if someone is forcibly trying to enter. And in the treasurer's office, the door blinds have been known to move.

The Ghost of Enos Kay

Timmons Covered Bridge Circa mid-1930s. Photo courtesy Nyla Timmons Holdren and the Vinton County Historical & Genealogical Society.

Enos Kay was 18 years-old in the spring of 1887. A handsome and popular boy, he had grown up in the fertile farmlands of Ross and Pickaway Counties near the towns of Mutton Jerk and Chillicothe, and then in the vicinity of Egypt Pike. But it was his 18th year that Enos fell hard in love with a pretty local girl by the name of Alvira. And she loved him dearly too. He would scrimp and save over the next two years, preparing for a wedding and a lifetime together. Between, the sweethearts would sneak away to be alone, meeting at local lover haunts like Timmons Covered Bridge just three miles from the Ross County line in Vinton County and other clandestine places away from prying eyes.

Timmons Covered Bridge at flood stage. Photo courtesy Nyla Timmons Holdren. More images of the bridge can be found in Images of America-Vinton County -Deanna L. Tribe with the Vinton County Historical Society.

But just a week before the couple would wed, a young man by the name of Mister Brown was invited to a church picnic that Enos and Alvira were also attending. Handsome, he was, and charming. So much so, he swept Alvira off her feet between bites of fresh summer pie. In just one warm afternoon, Enos was hardly a memory in the back of Alvira's mind. Two nights would pass. Alvira's new suitor shoved a ladder beneath her bedroom window and the two eloped.

Over the following days, Enos heard the awful whispers of the neighbors and clenched his teeth together. Anger, he felt. Heartbroken, he was. The two grievances so broiled together inside his soul, Enos Kay finally threw a fist into the air and vowed: "I'll kill myself and haunt fool lovers 'til the judgement day!"

And so, Enos did kill himself. Some accounts state he hanged himself from the very bridge rafters where he had met with Alvira. Others say it would be a bullet to his own head that brought Enos down. Regardless, the young man was dead. And it was only two days after he made his threat to haunt young lovers and then was buried in the ground that he made good his oath.

As a young couple paused beneath the Timmons Covered Bridge in their carriage, the top of their buggy came down with a snap. The horse started, his nostrils flared and his eyes opened wide. Then a hazy fog appeared above the carriage— the face of none other than Enos Kay!

Timmons Covered Bridge. Photo courtesy Nyla Timmons Holdren who grew up near the bridge.

Terrified, the couple would ride off into the night. But like others who felt the wrath of Enos Kay's vow through the years, the two lovers would always remember the terror they felt when the ghost of Enos Kay showed up within the bridge.

In fact, Nyla Timmons Holdren who grew up near the old covered bridge recalled a story her grandmother, Suzie Baker Timmons, once told to her. As a young woman Suzie Timmons was riding through the covered bridge at night when a dark shadowy figure grabbed a hold of the horse's bridle that was pulling her carriage. So startled was Miss Timmons that she gave a quick snap of her whip and the horse quickened his steps and got the carriage through. She never knew what had tried to seize the horse, but recounted the story to her children and grandchildren through the years.

Both the Timmons Covered Bridge and the old road where it once stood is long gone. The road is defunct and now runs into private property. The bridge was not used after 1953. However, don't worry. You only have to drive a few miles west for a ghostly treat. If you are looking for a scare, the legend states that Enos Kay will find any lovers who park in remote areas just over the line in Ross County!

Elmore Rider

Bridge over Big Mud Creek, south of Lindsey. Gift of Sarah Kroos

A ghostly tale comes from northern Ohio, 30 or so miles from Toledo near the towns of Lindsey and Elmore, about a couple who pledged their love to each other just as World War I broke out. The young man was sent off to war and fought overseas. The two wrote back and forth for a year, long letters of love and heartache and missing each other. Then the letters from the man simply stopped coming. Heartbroken, the young woman was sure her sweetheart had been killed.

It would be March 21st of 1918 when he returned from the war. Why he had not written his sweetheart, is not told. But to surprise the young woman as he neared her home, he shut off his motorcycle along the roadway the evening of his return and snuck to her window and peered inside. To his shock and dismay, the woman he thought pledged her life to him was with another man. Distraught, the young man shot off on his motorcycle down the road, not heeding his speed, nor ruts in the old farm road. Suddenly, he was thrown from his motorcycle near a small bridge over Muddy Creek. He flew from his bike and was decapitated by barbed fence wire running along the fields.

Now, legends tell that on March 21st of each year, the Elmore Rider returns. People standing near the bridge have seen a light slowly working its way down the roadway before it vanishes halfway across the bridge.

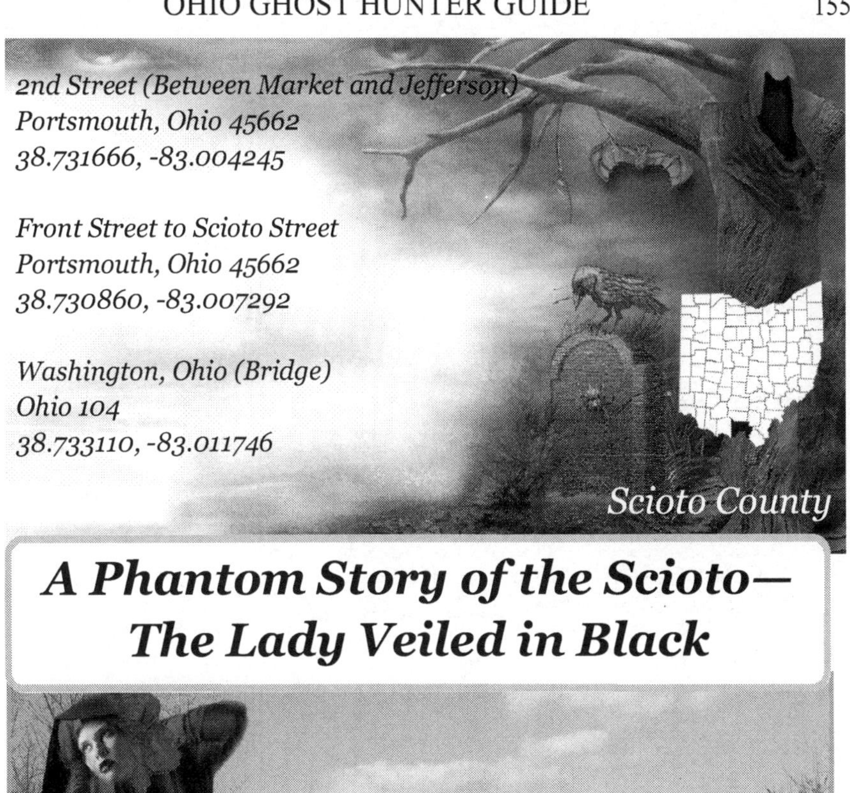

A Phantom Story of the Scioto—The Lady Veiled in Black

She wore the black clothing of mourning. A veil covered her face. To her bosom, she lovingly clasped a small child. The ghost they saw in Portsmouth making her way along Second Street, then into Front Street and lastly, to the Scioto Bridge floated eerily silent as if she was nothing more than wisps of fog caught in the flow of evening air wafting up from the Scioto River. Then, this ghost did something so horrid, so unpredictable it nearly brought grown men to their knees—

It was July 16th, 1888 in downtown Portsmouth. A certain stillness clung to the air with barely the hint of even the gentlest of breezes to dry the sweat settling like a clammy evening dew on the back of the neck. It was a hot and sticky Monday night with the kind of scents tinging the air that only river towns have when the wind blows just enough to barely nudge up air from the river below and along the streets above. But it was there, the faraway tang of dead fish, the sweet smell of moist algae and then the whiff of mist clinging to old rocks.

They were not the first to experience the ghost, but Nat Smith and Joe Henry saw it that night. The two were heading back to their farms near Carey's Run about 3 miles west of downtown Portsmouth after making several purchases in the city. Their trek home would take them along the interior of the city around Second Street, left on Jefferson Street until it met with Front Street which runs parallel to the Ohio River. Then, they would follow Front Street before taking a short jaunt north along Scioto Street where the Scioto River met the Ohio. There they would cross the Scioto River Bridge and work their way westward and home.

Front Street heading toward Scioto Street. The route that Nat Smith and Joe Henry took to follow the mysterious Lady in Black.

It was approximately 10 o'clock at night when the two farmers headed out. The already dim streets were only made darker by the thick foliage of the shade trees along the sidewalk. It was between Market and Jefferson Streets that Smith and Henry first felt a certain sensation of uneasiness. It was strange, this apprehension mixed with a bit of dread. Neither were unreasonably superstitious and they tried to shrug it off with nervous laughter. Perhaps it was nothing more than not looking forward to the four mile journey home. Because certainly they had passed by here many times before on dark nights heading home. Then again, there was one thing lingering on their mind. Just two weeks earlier, on July 1st, 1888 a laborer who lived in this very city by the name of Stephen Rayburn had been found dead by a milkman as he crossed over the Scioto Bridge. Rayburn's feet were barely visible among the rocks beneath the bridge, while his head was submerged in the Scioto. The local coroner considered the possibility Rayburn committed suicide, jumping from the fifty foot span to the rocks below, but marks on his skull appeared to have been made by a blunt object. Just the thought the crime had not been solved was enough to make any man take an extra peek over the shoulder where poor Rayburn had been murdered and wonder if his killer was still lurking about waiting for more prey along the river.

It was only a moment later when the *woman* appeared. She rushed past them in a swirl of icy wind that seemed to envelope the two, robed in mourning clothes—a dress of coarse, black material and a thick veil covering her face. Oddly, as her feet padded down the walkway, the sounds of her footsteps were unheard. The men watched in awed silence as she turned from Jefferson Street on to Front Street, nearly consumed in the shadows of the buildings. They hastened their steps, following the form that to their horror was floating like a cloth caught in the gentle breeze of the evening air.

She turned then, swept up Scioto Street. She was hardly an arms-length away from Misters Smith and Henry when she stepped on to the Scioto Bridge. There, she stopped where the middle span stood out from the water. Her eyes appeared to stare down into the depths below.

Scioto Street.

*. . . At Jefferson street the woman turned toward Front, crossing over and turning down Jefferson in the shadow of the buildings. The men, who were now thoroughly interested in the movements of the woman, followed her. Her progress was very slow, the form merely floating along with the evening air. This let the men ahead, and at the corner of Front they waited for the woman to pass. The same chilly experience was felt here, and the vision rushed on down the street. Smith and Henry followed. At the corner of Scioto street, the strange figure headed for the Scioto River bridge. When the men reached the bridge she was but a foot in front of them The same **AWE-INSPIRING DREAD** Was around them. Slowly the form floated along over the bridge until the middle span was reached, when it approached the railing, and, glancing over, peered intently at the water below. Smith and Henry stepped to the side of the bridge to await future movements. Scarcely had they done so when they were horrified to see the woman raise the child in her arms, and with a wild cry, dash it over the bridge. Both men turned in an instant and looked down at the water, but there was no break in its current, and nobody could be seen descending. Now thoroughly terrified, the men again looked up at the woman. For the first time her face was revealed. The heavy veil was thrown back and features sad, but singularly beautiful were shown. A second later the apparition ascended and gradually faded away, the men watching it in wonder until the **LAST FAINT OUTLINE DISAPPEARED** . . . SPECIAL DISPATCH TO THE ENQUIRER. Cincinnati Enquirer (Cincinnati, Ohio) July 17, 1888. WOMAN AND CHILD.*

Old Scioto Bridge. Courtesy of the Portsmouth Public Library, Portsmouth, Ohio. Historic Postcards

That was when the ghostly form raised up her arms. In her hands was the child and with a wild cry, she tossed it over the bridge. Utter horror overcame the men, nearly forcing them to keel over as they followed the tiny shape toward the dark current of the waters of the Scioto River and awaited for the splash to follow. And yet, no sound came to their ears. Both men looked up, followed the span between themselves and the woman who stood still before them. She tore back the veil covering her face and nothing but the sad, beautiful face of a woman stared back at them. She, then, faded away as if she was never there at all.

Those who lived in the vicinity of the streets along the river and those who crossed the bridge reported seeing the same apparition Nat Smith and Joe Henry saw that fateful Monday night. There were those who speculated the wandering woman in black may have something to do with the bridge collapse on May 21st, 1884. A Mrs. Fulwelier was walking with her four children across the bridge when it fell and three of the children were drowned. Others thought it may have to do with the murder of Stephen Rayburn. And yet, there was another conclusion. The previous winter, a mysterious woman had visited the Weber House (most likely a boarding house). She left most suddenly with her child and had never been heard from again.

Mault's Brewpub and the Portsmouth Brewing Company

Nathan Marshall, Brewmaster Assistant: At night, a shadowy figure wearing a fedora-like hat has been seen along the old alleyway where Nathan stands and is now the entrance to the brewery and shops.

A great place to get a beer, a pizza and maybe see a ghost —The Portsmouth Brewery is the oldest commercial brewery in Ohio and dates back to 1842-43. It's had some up and downs like belly-kicks from the Anti-Saloon League in the early 1900s, The Great Flood in 1913, and then Prohibition in 1919. Interestingly enough, the tunnel once existing between the river and the building is even thought to have been a part of the Underground Railroad.

Now it is a micro-brewery and restaurant. So a lot of people have passed through its doors and along the old alley that is enclosed in the center of the building now. Such . . . it shouldn't be surprising to find out from Will Mault and one of the brewmaster assistants, Nathan Marshall, that the building harbors a few spirited remnants of its past. And once in a while, old spirits and new patrons have crossed paths. A ghostly figure in a late-1800s fedora has been seen as a misty figure walking along the old bricks of the alleyway between the brewery and the restaurant. The jukebox that was once in the building would play only certain words in a song as if something was trying to communicate with customers. And there is a certain feeling you aren't alone when within the walls of the building's basement with its arches and bricked-in doorway once leading to the Scioto River.

Will Mault (right) talks about what's on tap at Mault's Brewpub at the brewery and relates a few stories he's heard over the years in the cellar that is being renovated. The cellar beneath the brewery once had an entrance to a tunnel leading to the river and the ice house. It was thought that perhaps this was used as part of the Underground Railroad for those escaping slavery from the south.

You may want to stop by there sometime and grab one of their homemade pizzas and hand-crafted beers (or a soda if you prefer). It makes for a great meal and maybe, while you're there, you might see a ghost!

Dead Man Hollow—Tinker's Tale

Dead Man Hollow where the ghost of a peddler from the 1800s haunts the hollow and surrounding roads.

It is an area of dense, dark forest in a secluded pocket of Scioto State Forest tucked between Little Gum Hollow and Webb Hollow. *Dead Man Hollow.* It is aptly named. A dead man was found here in 1824. No one knew who he was, only that he carried with him the wares of a pack peddler and tinker. . . combs, implements and tin plates, the type of things a traveling man would trade or the tools which he would use for those little repairs around the remote homes he stopped in on his way.

The crevice where it is believed the tinker's body was found, along Forest Road 2 and the bridle trail.

Many believed he was murdered. Andrew Lee Feight, Ph.D., with Scioto Historical, dug up some interesting information that came from Harry Knighton, a mycologist, who studied fungi in Shawnee State Forest. Knighton recounted that the peddler's bones and some miscellaneous supplies were found by CCC workers in the 1930s working on the forest roadway. It had been placed within the crevice of a small rock overhang. The body was later moved and reburied and a marker stone erected to commemorate the place.

In a newspaper article in the Monday May 31st, 1948 Portsmouth Times entitled: *Grave In the 'Wilds' Of Scioto Co Holds Secret* a local grocer in Friendship, Dan Stockum, related the story told to him by old-timers about the mysterious grave. It was believed that the peddler had paused in the town of Buena Vista in Scioto County, along the Ohio River. After selling his wares, he was directed about a 6 hour hike northeast to the settlement of Upper Turkey Creek. The now defunct community was about three miles north of the town of Friendship. His route would have been via a rugged foot path, up and down steep hills, between the two communities.

Along the way, it was speculated the peddler was ambushed and murdered, but no one really knew the truth *how* he died. Stockum stated that for many years, locals avoided the area after dark reporting it was haunted. A stone was set along the right fork of Twin Creek in the hollow to commemorate the peddler. It read: "H. T. Aug. 13, 1824. A. D., Dead M." After many years, flood waters along the Twin Creek washed the grave away and a bag of jewelry scattered nearby was discovered.

For many years, folks working their way along the gravel road would report ghostly screams, whistling and strange noises coming up from the belly of the hollow. A misty form walked the roadway, disappearing into deep brush along the creek bed.

Along the banks of Twin Creek where the peddler was buried.

Over the years, the markers placed by locals, CCC workers and forestry staff commemorating the tinker's death have been removed by vandals. Little remains to indicate where his body was discovered.

In an interview with Gilbert Roberts, local historian and former superintendent in the Cuyahoga Falls School system, a friend once confided in him about seeing a ghost on the Bailey Bridge in Cuyahoga Falls one night. The man, going by the name of Sam, was walking along the tracks as he came back from drinking with a friend. When the Capital Limited train from Akron came bursting through the darkness, the lights spilled across the tracks and then on to the bridge. Before him was a headless man in a long coat. He was leaning over the bridge.

Was it drunken imagination? Maybe, maybe not. He just may have seen the ghost. A ghost searching for its head, that is. Because there actually was a murder on the old bridge in April of 1853 and it ended with a headless corpse—

It was Wednesday, April 13th 1853. As the perfect precursor to any ghost story, it was a dark and stormy night. William Beatson, an Englishman and new to this country, had just come upon a large sum of money. Where the money came from can be left to the imagination. Most likely it was from a theft of some sort; although he was a butcher by trade, his reputation as a thief preceded him. But to those around him, he was quick to say he had earned the money selling a farm. He persuaded a man by the name of James Parks (aka James Dickinson), also from England, into taking a business trip to Pittsburgh with him.

Parks was a seedy character. Physically, he was described as being about 35 years-old, five foot and six inches, plump and missing his front teeth. He had spent time in jail in England for poaching, had been arrested for grave robbing there, too. Once in the United States and around 1841, he continued his career as a small-time criminal. Parks was jailed for grave robbing, escaping jail and finally convicted for burglary. Although he was never convicted of the crime, he was believed to have murdered his common law wife during this time.

By the early 1850s, James Parks was managing a shabby saloon on Pittsburgh Street in Cleveland. However, Parks had returned to England long enough to marry in January of 1853. Up until this point, he was known as James Dickinson. But his name and notoriety was beginning to haunt him. He changed his name then to James Parks. It was on the ship ride back to the United States that Parks met a man by the name of William Beatson. It was he who asked Parks to take the business train ride to Pittsburgh, Pennsylvania with him.

The two would seal their fate the day they headed off toward Pittsburgh. They never made it to their destination. Both had started drinking before they even left on the train. Beatson had been seen carrying a bottle of whiskey in his hand and was sufficiently drunk to be found dozing near a stove. Sometime during their ride, a call out was made for a change of cars. The two exited with Parks nearly dragging the soused Beatson along with him. Then they boarded the wrong train in Hudson and got out at the Falls Depot in Cuyahoga Falls.

It was believed the plan Parks had from the start was to rob Beatson of his money during the trip. Before the two hopped off the Pittsburgh-bound train, Parks had made an excuse he needed to grab a cap in one of his bags and surely went through Beatson's luggage searching for cash. Finding no money, Parks would opt for a different route to steal Beatson's cash, hence they "accidently" got off at Cuyahoga Falls. There, the two began to hit the taverns while they argued whether to walk the nearly eight miles back to Hudson or wait for another train. The rain was coming down heavily when the two made their way to Hall's Tavern, where they continued to drink until they were thrown out. It was the last time they would be seen together.

. . . They took the train for Cuyahoga Falls, where they stopped at Halls tavern. They drank there until refused liquor, Beatson drinking brandy and Parks beer. Parks said Beatson must go back with him to Hudson, as he had got him off the track, as Beatson wished to stay all night, and they were told at Halls that nothing could be gained by going before the morning train. They left the tavern, each smoking, and Beatson having filled his cigar-case. The conduct of Parks was such as to drag out from Hall the remark, that he (Parks) intended to rob Beatson, and that Beatson was so drunk as to leave his overcoat. On the next morning, half a mile from the tavern, where the railroad runs over the highway, blood was found; also a button from Beatson's vest, his cane, a strip from his stock, and his cap. Beatson's clothes were found in the canal; and on the second day, the headless body of Beatson was found, with a stab in the neck. ***Spirit of the Times. (Ironton, Oh) June 26, 1855.***

The next morning, two boys found pools of blood near Gaylord's Grove Bridge. A call out was made to local police and searchers immediately discovered items under the abutment of the bridge—a cane, a bottle, a button from Beatson's vest, a strip from his stock. . . and bits of brain. A cap was found on a stump in a nearby field. Beatson's slashed clothing was found in the Pennsylvania and Ohio Canal. Muddy footprints would lead to a canal. William Beatson's headless and naked body was discovered floating in the Cuyahoga River the next day. His head was never found.

It wasn't difficult tracing the murder to James Parks. He was found in Buffalo, New York. He was tried, convicted and hanged for his crime. Parks paid for his crime. William Beatson should be able to rest in peace. Or so it would be thought. There was just one problem. Beatson's head would never be found. And it is believed, he still searches for it today. He has been seen standing over the Bailey Road Bridge, staring at the Cuyahoga River, looking for his head.

The bridge where the ghost of Beatson still searches for his head.

The Everett Covered Bridge is the only remaining covered bridge in Summit County. It crosses Furnace Run and is part of the Cuyahoga Valley National Park system. The bridge was built in 1986 as an historically accurate duplicate of the original bridge lost in a flood in 1975.

It has a ghostly past. On a chilly Thursday afternoon in February of 1877, John Gilson and his wife were returning home after spending the day with friends. Their usual route, a ford across Furnace Run, was beneath ice and high waters from a winter snow. While crossing the stream, both were taken in by the waters. Missus Gilson was rescued by a boy happing past, but Mister Gilson drowned. His body was found four days later downstream.

The Stark County Democrat recounts the story:

At Boston peninsula, north of Akron a few miles, on last Thursday afternoon, while Mr. John Gilson and wife were attempting to cross Furnace Run their sligh (sleigh) upset and precipitated them into the water. Mrs. Gilson was rescued by a boy who happened to be near, but Mr. Gilson was carried out into the stream beyond his depth, and drowned. Mr. G. was sixty five years of age and an influential citizen. His body was found Sunday two miles down stream from where the accident occurred. Mr. G had in his pockets $1000 which was recovered uninjured. ***The Stark County Democrat, (Canton, Ohio) February 15, 1877.***

The date the original Everett Covered Bridge was built is unknown. There is some speculation it was built because of the horrible tragedy happening to the Gilsons. Another belief is that the bridge just might be haunted. The sound of horses pulling a carriage sleigh have been heard inside the bridge. Hooves make a faraway beat on the wood and the grumble of the weight of sleigh slipping through echoes on the walls.

Everett Covered Bridge Today—You can walk a gravel trail in the Cuyahoga Valley National Park along the same path others took long ago across the bridge .

Weird Visitors Outside Johnson's Corners—*Blazing Red Ball*

When folks in Canton sat down at the breakfast table on August 12th, 1902 they were in for a tantalizing treat. In the upper left corner of page 8 of the Stark County Democrat was published the following headline: **WEIRD VISITORS.** It was printed in bold, capitalized print. Beneath those words was written: **Linger In Vicinity of Dead Man's Home.**

It appears, the ghost of a dead man along with a mysterious-looking animal had returned to haunt a small farming community outside Johnson's Corner, Ohio. The ghost was that of 64 year-old John Shenaman who had died ten years earlier on June 19th, 1892. A little before Mister Shenaman's death, he sold a tract of his property to Carrara Paint Company in Barberton for a price of $6000.00. He died unexpectedly and his wife, Dora, would also pass away only 7 months later in January of 1893. His family searched frantically for this huge sum of money Mister Shenaman was thought to conceal around the home. They could only find $150.00 cash. Somewhere on the farm, there was money hidden. Yet, no one knew where it could be.

Johnson's Corner started with little more than a sawmill, store and tavern. It existed from 1817 until 1929 before being annexed into Barberton. Photo Courtesy: Thomas Conte, Akron Barberton Belt.

It was a quiet farming community of nice homes and crop fields where the ghost would first appear. County Commissioner John Breitenstine had purchased a bit of property nearby in 1888 from a Dr. Samuel Bargess along with a working coal mine on the back side of the property. John Shenaman and his wife Dora had lived right across the street. In fact, Mister Breitenstine was one of the first to witness the strange activity occurring at the Shenaman home. Upon the death of his neighbor, as was customary at the time, several people "stayed up with the corpse," watching over it to keep rodents away from the body before burial. Mister Breitenstine and two of his neighbors were doing just that when a light appeared in the corner of the room.

Akron, O., Aug. 11.- A ball of fire, which hovers over the locality in which lived the late John Shaneman and a mysterious animal which vanishes into thin air when pursued, are causing a commotion in Norton township, says a special to the Cleveland Plain Dealer. It is said these weird objects represent the spirit of Shaneman returned to earth to try to show relatives where he concealed his fortune. Shaneman was a farmer and although he lived very frugally, he was reckoned well to do. . . ***The Stark County Democrat., (Canton, Ohio) August 12, 1902, WEEKLY EDITION, Page 8. Weird Visitors.***

Breitenstine recounted the following:

"We never saw any of these strange things before the death of Shaneman, and the first time I saw anything supernatural was the night after Shaneman's death. Peter Shaffer, John Mong and myself were sitting up with the corpse. Mong was smoking, and Shaffer and I had been talking. All of a sudden Shaffer gave me a little nudge and directed my gaze to the celling at the corner of the room where the corpse lay, when I saw a sight that fairly made my hair stand on end. What seemed a ball of fire had started from the corner of the room and was traveling slowly around the ceiling of the room, "Did you see it?" said Shaffer.

"Yes," said I.

"Let's get out of here," were Shaffer's next words, and we made for home as fast as we could. And since that time the strange light has haunted this vicinity with the most unpleasant regularity. . . ***Interview by Akron daily Democrat., August 08, 1902, Page 2. Blazing Red Ball***

It wouldn't be the last time the ghost would show up. The light was as bright as a large streetcar headlight when it glared into John Breitenstine's bedroom window some nights. It would slip up from the farm fields behind the Shenaman's home or alight on the roof of the house. Peter Shaffer, father of a boy and two girls and also a local coal miner lived near the Breitenstine's. Once while the Shaffer family was visiting with the Breitenstine family on the front porch, the light bloomed across the road and slipped down the lane right next to the silent crowd gaping at it until it disappeared behind a barn. They jumped up to chase it and just as the pursuers were upon the light, it simply vanished.

The light was so brilliant at times, it would appear a building was on fire. Shaffer's grown son would come running from his farm calling an alarm about the house being on fire. It was even known to chase Peter Shaffer's screaming wife and daughters across a field. And if the ghostly light was not enough to haunt the neighborhood, there was a strange wolf-like animal that seemed to come right after Shenaman's death. Peter Shaffer's daughters, 23 year-old Louisa and 21 year-old Minnie watched terrified as a strange animal appeared in front of them on a dark walk home one night and twined its way between their legs. They tried to hit it with sticks, then sprinted home, nearly too shaken to tell their story.

John Breitenstine's 28 year-old son, Harry, then grown and moved into the old Shenaman homestead, saw the light quite often. John's 13 year-old son, Newton, watched in disbelief once as an old apple tree in the yard became alit with a thousand tiny glowing lights of all colors. With a blanched face, he walked to the door where his mother was within, "Oh, ma, Come here!" he could barely whisper. As Sarah Breitenstine came to the doorway and peered outside, she too saw the lights before suddenly, they flit away down the lane toward an orchard.

Peter Shaffer related to the Akron Daily Democrat that about 4 o'clock one afternoon, he was heading toward Adam Kiehl's coal mine on the rear of Breitenstine property to pick up a load of coal. As he neared it, he saw someone along the incline of the mine. Believing it to be a worker, Shaffer stopped to hail the man for the order. Strangely, though, the person was making their way up the mine on all fours before stopping on the platform. Thinking someone was going to play a practical joke on him, Shaffer attempted to approach, but when doing so saw the form was not a man at all, but a strange gray animal that disappeared into the mine. A few days later two Barberton locals working at the mine saw the same peculiar beast. In terror, they took off after it with their mining picks. However, as they struck at the animal, it would vanish.

The Breitenstine and Shenaman farms were along what is now between the park and where Eastern Road meets with 31st Street SW.

The Shenaman property would be home to different families over time. As the years passed, some would see the lights. Others would not. The Breitenstines and Shaffers would always hold their heads high and attest to the fact they saw the ghostly lights and the strange gray animal. Some would believe the stories. Others would not. Perhaps you can see the ghostly lights too. Part of the old Breitenstine property is now Breitenstine Park. The mine and homes are gone, but the ghost of Shenaman may still be flitting around and waiting for someone to find his money.

Weeping Woman of Lock 3

The Ohio and Erie Canal traversed Ohio from Portsmouth to Cleveland, connecting many of the northern and southern cities when carriage, foot and horseback were the only options for travel. It prospered from the 1830s to the 1860s and served Akron from 1827 until 1913. Then, with the Great Flood of 1913, city workers had to dynamite the locks to rid the excess debris and water threatening downtown.

Remnants of Akron's canal years still remain, though, tucked here and there like Akron's Lock 3, the third lock of 24 in Akron. Perhaps there is a ghost left behind too. Visitors report seeing a woman in white crying near the lock.

On November 27th, 1955, five teenage girls carried out an escape from the Summit County Juvenile Detention Home by overpowering the matron, Eula Bonham, who had entered their dormitory on the second floor for a routine nightly inspection. Police reported that the girls tied her with belts from their dresses and gagged her with ammonia soaked rags stuffed into her mouth. Eula died from suffocation. The girls would escape, but later faced prison terms for manslaughter.

Both inmates in the detention home and jail workers have experienced ghostly activity there now. They believe it is Eula still monitoring the halls. Windows are said to open and close and electrical appliances turn off and on.

Captain Nathaniel Bettes was in the Revolutionary War and served beneath George Washington. For his service, he was given 500 acres of land in the Akron area which he settled in 1810. He called it Bettes Corner.

When Captain Bettes died in 1840 at age 93, he was buried in the Bettes Cemetery. Others came before him and others would follow. But none have been buried in the old cemetery in over 50 years. It stands tucked into an alcove between buildings, nearly hidden from the world. Still, shadows have been seen there, flitting around the old pioneer cemetery's stones. They are perhaps just another remnant of the city's past hoping to blend with the present before their headstones vanish into the soil and their memories are completely gone.

It was right around suppertime—6 p.m. on July 31st, 1940. Pennsylvania Railroad's Motor Car 4648, a gas-powered shuttle rail-car called the Doodlebug was running between Akron and Hudson. Just as a 73-car freight train crossed the Front Street intersection in Cuyahoga Falls, the Doodlebug collided with it head-on. The evening was shattered by the explosion. Nine passengers were killed on impact. Thirty-four of the passengers burned to death when a gasoline tank ruptured on impact, spraying the interior of the coach with flaming gas.

On some nights, you can hear the ill-fated rail car making its way down the tracks. Some people have crossed paths with unsettled ghosts from the wreck. They appear to be confused as they make their way along the track seemingly unsure they are dead or where they are going.

Mary Campbell was a 10 year-old girl from Pennsylvania who was kidnapped by the Delaware Indians around 1758. Red-haired and freckle-faced, she was held captive at Chief Newcomer's village near Old Maid's Kitchen, a cliff overhang in Gorge Metro Park in Cuyahoga Falls. She was later returned to her family and died around 1801.

Some believe she spent time in the cave, thus the title it was given—Mary Campbell Cave. Some also believe spirits of Native Indians, including a young girl that looks quite like Mary with her freckles and red hair, haunt the cave. Tiny lights have been known to dance along the trail. Whistling, children singing, and laughter echo through this recess cave.

The Mountain Line was an open-sided trolley car running from Main Street in Akron to its destination in Cuyahoga Falls. Along the route and just before it reached its final stop on Front Street, the Mountain Line would cross over the Glen Bridge, a bridge running about 100 feet over the Cuyahoga River.

On the warm Tuesday afternoon of June 11th, 1918, Mountain Line Trolley Car #350 made a quick stop on the eastern side of the bridge to let off a couple passengers. It then began a slow journey across the bridge. Unknown to Leroy Bessemer, the motorman and O. D. Gilmore, the conductor, the front wheels of the car had come off the track. Unable to hold up the weight of the car, the wooden planks and railing gave way. The trolley fell quickly to the Cuyahoga River below.

Wreck of the Mountain Line Trolley-The rescue. Photo courtesy: http://mredmountainline.blogspot.com/

PROBE TROLLEY CRASH WHICH KILLED FOUR

Akron, Oh --Three separate investigations were under way today in an effort to fix the blame for the Mountain Line trolley accident late yesterday which resulted in the death of four persons and serious injury to two others. . . The Glens Bridge, where the car left the rails, is 100 feet above the bed of the Little Cuyahoga river. The car landed bottom up in the bed of the stream. The four dead were instantly killed. ***Lima Daily News June 12, 1918. PROBE TROLLEY CRASH WHICH KILLED FOUR***

For years after the accident, when the water in the Cuyahoga River became low, you could see fragments of the wreck still sitting on the rocks below. Rumors persist that if you stand on the bridge, you may feel the vibrations of the car that fell over that fateful day. Voices, low and far below, conjure up images of the spirits who died there.

A memorial for the disaster site can be visited today.

Indian Signal Tree

Native Indians forced hardwood trees to grow in certain shapes for use as signals on a trail. By bending a sapling limb and holding it down by some means, they could force it to grow at an angle.

The Indian Signal Tree in the Chuckery Area of Summit Metro Parks is a Burr Oak used in this way. It marked a portage path between the Cuyahoga and Tuscarawas Rivers. It is believed to be 300 years old and quite possibly, haunted. The sound of voices has been heard near the tree and tiny lights have been seen dancing around its canopy.

Old Summit County Home

The Summit County Home in Tallmadge opened in 1921 and remained a safe harbor for the poor, those with mental illnesses and the elderly until 1970. In 1980, the building was demolished. The cemetery for the county home and indigent graves from the city of Akron and Summit County, remains, however, with graves from about 1916 to 1948. Most of the stones are long gone. Ghosts are still here, though. You may be able to see them while you hike beautiful Munroe Falls Metro Park. Watch for lights bobbing in the evening air and misty apparitions within the confines of the cemetery.

Botzum in its heyday. Photo Courtesy: Summit Memory, Portage Lakes Historical Society Collection.

The old ghost town of Botzum started as a canal town along the Yellow Creek Basin in the 1820s and managed to stay alive for nearly a century. Back in the early canal days, the town was initially named Yellow Creek Basin. Around 1835, the Botzum family would move into the area, settling into farm life and watching the town around them grow. And it did. As the railway came through, John Botzum became the station agent of the village. The depot was then called Botzum Station and the town was rechristened Botzum. In its heyday, it boasted a general store, hotel, tavern, saloon, post office, school, sawmill, railroad station, covered bridge, blacksmith shop, mill, boatyard, warehouses and homes.

Botzum Depot—You can walk through part of the town of Botzum along the Ohio & Erie Canal Towpath Trail in Cuyahoga Valley National Park—2812 Riverview Road, Akron Ohio.

During the 1880s, Seth Thomas managed the Botzum boarding house in a building that had, for many years, been used as the Yellow Creek Basin Hotel. One of its unique features was a large ballroom on an upper floor that was still greatly used for entertainment around the region. He had a 22 year-old daughter, Ellen, who made her home there too.

On the night of October 27th, 1882 Ellen was one of the 20 or so young couples who had gathered in the country tavern ballroom. They had assembled from all over the community for the much-anticipated social event of the season. Young people from Botzum and neighboring communities had come together for a dance to the tunes of the local Buckeye Cornet Band, a group of young local men who were showing off their musical talents with a social dance.

The night should have held nothing more than amusement for the young people, one of them being a young Englishman by the name of Thomas Brook. Thomas had lived in the village a few years and worked as a tenant with his brother on the Botzum farm. Described as short-statured, but strongly built, the 24 year-old man was vying heavily for the affections of Miss Ellen Thomas.

All was going well into the evening until a local farmhand by the name of John Tedrow entered the hotel, drunk and ready to cause a fight. Tedrow was a tall and muscular man, about 25 to 30 years of age. Newspaper accounts would note that he could be a pleasant man when he wasn't drinking, but most of the time, he was drunk. An alcoholic, he was quite quarrelsome and bullying and had previous run-ins with the law in the region.

After taking a quick supper at the hotel, Tedrow and several friends visited a local saloon. Then as the dancing began at the hotel, he returned and began accosting the guests and loudly yelling obscenities in the ballroom. "I can lick anybody in the room!" he had called out. Then Tedrow set his sights on the boarding house manager, Seth Thomas, by aggressively grabbing his clothing and pushing and pulling him back and forth. Not long after, Tedrow knocked the young Thomas Brook from the porch and fell atop him, tearing his coat.

There seemed to be a moment when the storm brewing would simply fade away. Tedrow disappeared down the road, irritable but seemingly deflated, returning to the saloon and leaving the young dancers to enjoy their evening. During this time, Thomas Brook sent Charles, a 16 year-old son of Seth Thomas, to fetch Ellen and Mabel Gray, one of his sister-in-laws, to return to the kitchen to mend his torn coat. The coat was mended; the happily chattering young people set their sights on the dance floor once again.

It was 11 p.m. All four were returning to the dance when they were surprised by Seth Thomas running through the door with Tedrow cursing and in angry pursuit. Tedrow skidded to a halt before Thomas Brook readying to confront the younger man. But just as he did, Ellen pushed between the two trying to stop Tedrow from hitting the young man. She snatched at his collar and began to speak. But Thomas Brook grabbed an axe that Seth Thomas handed him and hit John Tedrow on the head. The blow instantly killed him.

Murder at Akron -Akron, O., October 28-John Tedrow, colored, was killed at Botzum's Station by Thomas Brooks, white, aged twenty-four years. Tedrow was in Akron in the afternoon and got drunk, and when he returned to Botzum he was in a quarrelsome mood. About 9 o'clock Tedrow went to a ball room, where he had a squabble with several persons, Brooks being of the number. Subsequently, about 11 o'clock, Brooks and Tedrow met in the hallway, when Brooks struck Tedrow with an axe, felling him to the floor. Tedrow died almost instantly. The morning, before daylight, Brooks surrendered to the authorities. . . . ***The Wheeling Daily Intelligencer. (Wheeling, W Virginia) October 30, 1882. Murder at Akron***

Thomas Brook was charged with murder and spent three years in the penitentiary. He paid for his act in the murder and returned to a quiet life in Cleveland. Miss Ellen Thomas would try to forget the horrid night and would marry another several years later. The bustling town of Botzum would fade away to nothing more than the quiet old foundation stones sticking out of tall grass.

John Tedrow, however, can't seem to find peace. As he was angry and quarrelsome in life, he appears to be restless in death. Frantic footsteps can be heard running from where the old hotel once stood and his ghost can be seen slipping through the woods.

Little remains but old foundations where Botzum's town center and the hotel stood. And John Tedrow's irritable ghost.

Strange Light Along the Border-A Bloodcurdling Ghost Story

A ghostly apparition began appearing in the autumn of 1885 to local farmers living along the Ohio and Pennsylvania borders. It was described as a light, twice the size of a lantern, that would change from a pretty blue tint to red, then bright yellow. It would glide along the hills about six feet above the ground, disappearing at the old Rock Ridge Cemetery just across the state line in Pennsylvania.

Newspapers across the state published this story in connection with the apparition:

In the mid-1800s, the Ohio towns of Burgh Hill and Vernon along Trumbull County's Pennsylvania border were growing villages with prosperous farmers between.

One such farmer was John Harbush who had land along the road just outside Vernon, Ohio. Living with Mister Harbush was his daughter, Mary, a beautiful young woman who was known for her kindness and sweet nature. It was only the two of them, the girl's mother dying long before. So Mister Harbush was quite protective of his only child. She had many men wishing to court her, but her father had already chosen a husband for Mary. This man was quite rich, had many cattle and was much older than the girl.

Mary would have none of this. She had fallen in love with an outgoing, popular teacher, Richard Lewis, from Pennsylvania. Each night after all were in bed, the two would sneak out and meet at a hilly meadow nearby the Rock Ridge Cemetery just over the state line.

The star-crossed sweethearts were destined for tragedy. And so it was not long before the man who had been chosen by her father to court her caught wind of the clandestine affair between Mary and Richard. He stormed into the home of Mister Harbush and demanded something be done. John Harbush held out his hand, bid the angry man to be patient. He would take care of the situation. So he did. He waited out his time, watched his daughter leave the house at night and followed her down Burgh Hill-Vernon Road, then along the road leading toward Greenville before she turned along State Line Road.

The two sweethearts would walk the nearby State Line Road and meet in the meadow at Rock Ridge Cemetery.

Mary slipped past the Rock Ridge Cemetery and walked up the path to a small hill. Just as the two embraced, Harbush charged forward, striking Lewis on the head. The young teacher died instantly from the wound. Mary sank to her knees next to her sweetheart, screaming an echo that reverberated through the hills. Shock overwhelmed her and she fell nearly senseless atop the dead man. John Harbush carried his daughter home in his arms, but not before hiding the body of the young man.

It is said when she awakened the next morning, her hair was nearly white. But Mary never spoke of her father's murder, simply remained silent for her remaining days. She needn't keep the secret long. Mary died only three months later and took the horrid killing to her grave.

After the death of his daughter, Harbush took to drinking. His farm fell into disrepair and he died not long after. But on his dying bed, he admitted to killing Richard Lewis. However, he did not tell anyone where he was buried. But people knew. Because in the winter of 1882, farmers along the Pennsylvania and Ohio border began witnessing a light hovering along the roadways near their property and working its way to and from the old Rock Ridge Cemetery just over the Pennsylvania line. It was twice the size of a lantern flame, would change colors and slink its way along State Line Road, sweep out to a small hill, then return and disappear again in the Rock Ridge Cemetery.

A light has been seen floating in the Rock Ridge Cemetery.

The area newspapers like the Elyria Republican and the Summit County Beacon had this to say about the light:

. . . But the strangest part of the story is yet to be told. For several months past the people of that neighborhood have been greatly mystified by the appearance of a strange, brilliant light. It is about twice as large as the flame made by a lantern, and is changeable in hue. At one time it is of a pretty blue tint, and at another a bright red, and sometimes a pale yellow. It seems to rise in the burial ground, glides or floats gently down one hill-always at a uniform distance of about six feet from the ground-up the other hill, and hovers for a few minutes in the locality of the supposed grave of the murdered man. It always returns, however, and disappears in the old Rock Ridge Cemetery. Sometimes it goes beyond the meadow and disappears in the woods for a short time, reappearing, however, and after lingering in the neighborhood goes out of sight among the tombstones. The strange light has no regular time for coming, somethings putting in an appearance as early as 9, and at intervals between that and 1 in the morning.

The meadow in question is owned by David Stull, he having purchased it of the heirs of James Harbush. One evening Mrs. Mark Doyle was returning from church, and noticing the light supposed it was one of her neighbors carrying a lantern, and who was taking a short cut home. The lady followed the mysterious illumination, when it led her into a deep wood, and suddenly went out of sight, leaving Mrs. Doyle, almost frightened to death, to find her way out as best she could. When she finally groped her way to the edge of the woods, she saw it hovering over a certain spot in the fateful meadow.

Mr. George Foulk, a well-to-do farmer, has often witnessed the strange spectacle, as have also David Stull, Mark Doyle, and dozens of other residents in that vicinity. To say the least the inhabitants are mystified, as well they might be. A movement has been organized to find out, if possible, what the strange thing really is. Each farmer has provided himself with a large bell, and whoever sees the light first will apprise his neighbors by violently ringing the bell. It will be surrounded and if possible hemmed in, when the virtue of powder and ball in solving the mystery will be tested. ***Elyria Republican. (Elyria, Ohio) January 29, 1885. A Blood Curdling Story***

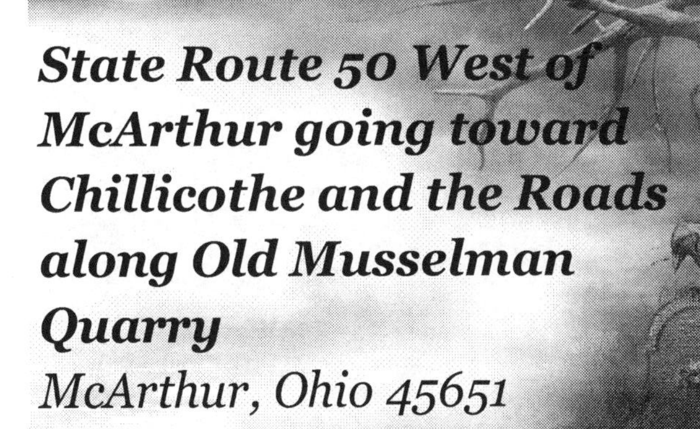

State Route 50 West of McArthur going toward Chillicothe and the Roads along Old Musselman Quarry

McArthur, Ohio 45651

Vinton County

Legend of the Murdered Peddler

". . . Tradition holds an unwritten account of the most cruel murder of a peddler, who brought the first two-wheel vehicle ever seen in this section. It is so traditional that we will only mention that the story recites—that he was decapitated with a broad-axe his body secreted, all except a bearded strip of his neck, which was supposed to have been left on the log where he was executed by a second blow of the axe; tradition further says that the wheels of his cart were found in a deep ravine west of the (now) Sinnott farm. We do not vouch for the truth of this particular part of this sketch, further than we have heard it oft repeated in our childhood days. But we will guess that had some one driven an auto to the (then) Musselman quarry, unloaded a phonograph, and let loose its record to sing a song, —that those pioneer lads, brave as they were of the dangers of dense forests, yes, we will guess they would have "took" to the deeper woods more frightened than to have seen the murdered peddler's ghost, which they said did walk the road at night. . . ***Republican Enquirer. (McArthur, Ohio) March 29, 1920. Vinton County. 114 Years Ago in Vinton County History, By Our Route 2 Correspondent.***

Peddlers were a welcome sight in rural towns in the 1800s. Traveling the backroads to get to remote homesteads like those in McArthur, though, made the peddlers easy prey for thieves. Photo courtesy: Library of Congress.

In 1806, the southeastern part of Ohio was thick with wilderness. It had yet to be torn asunder by timbering, iron furnaces, and strip mining. Settlers were just beginning to put up little, crude cabins here and there where the sun poked through to grassy meadows between the slim wagon path between Athens and Chillicothe. Grist mills and grocers were few and far between. Pack peddlers worked their way along the mucky roads and trails, going from homestead to homestead to sell their wares to owners eager to obtain products from the outlying cities that appeared so far away before cars seemed to bring them closer.

It was the spring of this year that all began to change in the little pocket of Vinton County. A miller and geologist from Philadelphia who had moved to the area by the name of Musselman discovered buhrstone (a mix of flint, quartz and limestone used to make millstones) west of what is now McArthur and began operating a quarry. Within a few years Isaac Pierson took over. McArthur soon became a productive quarry boomtown—stones were sent all over the U.S. By the early 1820s, the quarry employed 14 men and 2 women who shaped the buhrs. As the Musselman prospered and more quarries were established, folks began to settle the area, and start tiny farms to supplement their income.

The rugged roads around the area where the land was once quarried like Route 50, Locust Grove and Township Road 17, shown, don't appear much different today as they did 200 years ago. . . except there is less traffic.

It was in these early days, about 1817, a peddler came to town. At this time, there were about 50 or so families living in Elk Township where the quarries were worked. Taking a wagon to buy needed items at the closest town like Chillicothe or Athens was a thirty mile trip one way along a rutted path barely excusable as a road and would take most of the day. Such, peddlers with carts loaded with essential items were a welcome sight. However, they were also easy prey for robbers and thieves who would hide in the miles of remote and dark recesses and steal the money the lone peddlers had collected selling their wares.

This was the case with one peddler who had stopped in the town of McArthur and had worked his way among those living near the Musselman Quarry about a mile and a half on the outskirts of the new town. Those living in the area of McArthur described him as an attractive man and his face was framed in a "throat whisker," a heavy beard. He had a newfangled horse and buggy filled with table cutlery, silver spoons, lace and material for sewing and some special treats for children. He was originally from Pennsylvania and was very kind. The peddler was quick to win over the quarry workers and their families with his wit and charm.

In fact, he made himself so welcome, the peddler was able to stay beneath the townspeople's roofs for a few nights while he sold his wares along the old road furrowed deep with ruts from the wagons between Athens and Chillicothe and across the settlement, up and down the rugged hills from farm to farm. Then, quite suddenly, he disappeared . .

An early peddler with a two-wheeled cart.

. . .On his last trip he seemingly disappeared as completely as if the earth swallowed him up. One wheel of his buggy was found by a hunter in a deep ravine in a clump of hazel bushes and various were the speculations as to his utter disappearance until some of the settlers made a ghastly discovery.

On the high ridge east of the quarry there had been a great oak cut down for the purpose of hewing out its great body a shaft for the overshot wheel for a mill. This tree grew near the Chillicothe-Athens trail which was bordered on both sides by dense woods. The shaft had been hewn out and removed for several weeks. One of the workmen had forgotten his broad axe at the time of the removal of the shaft and had returned to get it. He found the broad axe near where he had left it, but with its finding made the discovery of blood stains on the log and found the marks of the axe where two blows had been struck, the last of the two as it was thot (thought) had severed a piece of the throat which lay on the log and which bore the whiskers once worn by the peddler.

This discovery ended the speculation as to how the peddler had come to an end—probably as one of the settlers remarked—"they were afeared to shoot on account of the rifle crack—they've brained him and to make sure of the job axed his head off." ***Athens Sunday Messenger March 11, 1923 The Legend of the Musselman Quarry. A Story of 1817. By George Benson Dillon***

After the gory find of the remains of the peddler, ghost stories began to spread throughout the hills and valleys around McArthur and its quarries. A ghost of a man without a head walked the trails around the Musselman Quarry and along the road between Athens and Chillicothe.

George Benson Dillon, a teacher and a reporter for the Athens Messenger in the 1920s, once told a story his father related to him. His father, John Dillon, was a shoemaker in the mid-1800s in McArthur. One evening after repairing a neighbor's boots in his home, Mister Dillon bid the other man goodnight and sent him on his way. The path the neighbor had to take was along the ridge that was haunted by the peddler's ghost. It was not long after the neighbor left, when he returned in nearly a state of shock, banging on the door of Mister Dillon.

It seems the apparition of a woman appeared before him, 40 feet tall. When he tried to fend her off with blows, his fists went right through her body. And she refused to allow him to pass. Years later, a woman and two men came to McArthur. They had little boxes with arrows in them that they claimed would point to the grave of the dead peddler. It seems a silver plate had once been placed inside the dead man's body and the arrow would detect where he had been buried. However, when the trio took their equipment to a certain, unnamed farm in the county, the farmer turned the woman away with a wave of his rifle, refusing her on his property. The lady did not say a word other than she was the peddler's daughter and upon the farm they tried to identify the grave, there was an unmarked burial place. However, they would never know if it was the place the peddler was buried or who had murdered him.

The buhrstone quarrying around McArthur ended around 1860. But the ghost of the peddler lived on in legend for much longer, returning to the roadways around the old Musselman Quarry just west of the city proper.

Most of these old roads are long gone with the quarries, buried beneath years of strip mining. White signs with black writing screaming PRIVATE PROPERTY and NO HUNTING are tacked lopsided on trees on either side of the roads.

But of those few old traces of quarry roads that are left, like State Route 50 outside McArthur, the dead peddler still walks them. Old legends tell he works his way along the old dirt wagon paths between that have hardly changed with time except a layer of pebbles has been added by township road crews to help modern car and tractor tires from digging too deep into the mud while they make their way down the street.

The peddler is said to be a solitary figure darker than the night and still pushing his cart. Those who dare to take the old roads once surrounding the quarry may still see the peddler there or hear his heartrending cries that are reported to send chills down the spine and hair standing on end.

Ghostly Remnants of Lost Love

The Buckley House was originally a private residence built in 1879 for one of the wealthier citizens of Marietta, Miss Maria Morgan Woodbridge. Considered quite pious, she was unmarried and living alone in 1881. It was in the early 1880s, she sponsored a young man from Canton, China to come to Marietta College to study theology in the hopes he would return to his country as a missionary for the church. William New Kim, 26 years-old and a second-year student in the preparatory department of Marietta College had been converted to Christianity in China and brought over by the Woodbridge family.

During his stay, he fell madly in love with a 21 year-old German housemaid, Sophia Hoff, working for Miss Woodbridge. She, too, fell in love with the young man. Knowing their love may not be accepted by those around them, the two were married secretly in a practice accepted by his culture, by pledging their love to each other as man and wife before consummating the marriage. Not long after, Sophia was sent to Cincinnati by Woodbridge. The couple would remain faithful for some time, sending each other letters of love. However, it was not long before Miss Woodbridge found out about the two lovers and the woman chastised William New Kim for living in such sin. She brought in a local minister to counsel the young man on his impropriety. Kim became quite distraught, believing he had shamed his family with this sin Miss Woodbridge pinned on him. Within a few days, he purchased a bottle of chloroform, dressed for burial and committed suicide in his bed.

WM. NEW KIM, known as Ab. Kim, a Chinese missionary, student in the second year of the preparatory department of Marietta college, at Marietta, Ohio, committed suicide by use of cloral or chloroform last Monday, and was found dead in his bed. His trouble was disappointment in a love affair with a servant girl in that city. ***Bismarck tribune., (Bismarck, ND) November 11, 1881***

Such tragedies spurn unrest in spirits. And some believe William New Kim's heartbreak and suicide have left their mark on the old Woodbridge home. Although it is an upscale restaurant now, it was once a bed and breakfast stay. During this time and over the years, those staying in the upstairs have heard doors opening and shutting, the sound of footsteps and felt cold spots.

Ghostly Flames of Colonel William Crawford

William Crawford was a soldier in both the French and Indian War and the American Revolutionary War during the 1700s. In 1782 and toward the end of the Revolutionary War, he led an expedition of about 500 volunteers against Indian villages along the Sandusky River, hoping to surprise them. Unfortunately for Crawford, word had spread of his attack and tempers were high. In March of the same year, American militia had cruelly massacred 96 peaceful Delaware at a missionary village in Gnadenhutten.

In June just south of where the town of Carey now stands, the Indians along with their British allies met Crawford's troops with 440 of their own men. Crawford and many of his men were captured. Shortly after the defeat, it was learned that some of Crawford's men had been a part of the Gnadenhutten massacre. As a result, Crawford was brutally tortured by the Indians for over two hours, then burned with ashes and sticks.

It was along the valley of Tymotchee creek in Northwestern Wyandot County that Colonel William Crawford was burned at the stake. It was the 11th day of June, 1782. Although no one knows the exact spot where Crawford was burned, old accounts and old maps suggest it was at a point called High Bank along the Tymotchee Creek near the old Buell farm (40.923062, -83.334445) which is on private property now. However, Ron Marvin with the Wyandot County Historical Society has researched in great depth the history behind the Crawford killing. He reveals that perhaps the actual site is, in reality, closer than once believed to the monument dedicated to William Crawford in the Ritchy cemetery and near the creek shore.

But it is also here that as settlers began to pour in during the early 1800s, strange events began to occur. On some nights along the banks of the Tymochtee where Crawford was burned to death, the apparition of a man would be seen hovering around. It was enveloped in a circle of fire.

> *A dispatch from Upper Sandusky to the Enquirer says: "Some queer stories have been floating around this town for some time to the effect that a strange apparition is to be seen of nights out on the banks of the Tymochtee in the vicinity of the place where Colonel Crawford was burned to death by the Indians almost a century ago. The form of a human being is seen or said to be seen moving about, inclosed in a circle of fire, and of course the conclusion is arrived at that it is the ghost of Colonel Crawford. Just what has raised it doesn't appear to be definitely settled."* ***Democratic Northwest.,(Napoleon, Ohio) August 02, 1888.***

Haunted Hocking is based out of the Hocking Hills, so we have an insider's look at some of the best places for ghost hunters to visit. The Hocking Hills region offers a unique place to visit, especially if you like to actually get out and explore haunted places. There are plenty of cabins to rent so you can stay a few nights and check out all the ghostly areas.

All Hocking Hills State Parks like Ash Cave and Old Man's Cave close at dusk and are patrolled so ghost hunting at night is prohibited. However, most ghostly experiences there have been during the daylight or evening hours. There have also been naturalist-guided ghost hunts after dark.

Old Man's Cave

Old Man's Cave - Hocking Hills State Park

19852 Ohio 664

Logan, OH 43138

39.426656, -82.536369

Old Man's Cave *(also once known as Dead Man's Cave): Old Man's Cave is a popular tourist attraction in southeastern Ohio featuring a hiking trail that winds through a long, tree-lined gorge with cliff edges, waterfalls and unique rock formations.*

Haunted by the ghost of a trapper who made his home within the gorge. His ghost is said to walk the trails, even stopping long enough to curiously stare at people. His hound dog can be heard during the evening and at night baying. This has been heard by people night fishing at Rose Lake and camping in the Hocking Hills State Park campground.

Newspapers in the very early 1900s reported that those who saw the old man along the trail stated he appeared just as clear to them as a live person. He was an elderly, bearded man in old-fashioned clothing, carrying a flintlock rifle on his shoulder and leading a white dog.

It was only when the old man walked to the ledge of the cave where the body of a trapper was found by two boys in the 1800s and vanished into a mist did they realize it was not a man. Although it has been perpetuated in late-1900s articles that the trapper's name was Richard Roe, early newspaper articles suggest quite differently. When the body was first found, an epitaph had been written above the grave: Retzler (the trapper's name), Harper (the hound dog), and Pointer (the name of the man's rifle.) The date engraved on the gun was that of 1702. The old man died in 1777.

Ash Cave

Ash Cave— Hocking Hills State Park

State Route 56

South Bloomingville, Ohio 43152

39.396093,-82.545969

Ash Cave *features a winding, asphalt hiking trail ending in Ohio's largest recess cave with a high, seasonal waterfall. One great feature of the cave is that the trail leading back to it is wheelchair accessible and such, provides easy access for ghost hunters with limited mobility.*

The ghost of a young woman dressed in 1920s clothing has been seen along the trail that winds its way to the waterfall at Ash Cave. She has been seen peering from behind trees and has been known to tag along on guided night hikes, easing back just far enough to appear like one of the group until she fades away.

No one has pinpointed who the ghostly woman might be. However, Ash Cave has been long used for church services – there is a large, flat rock just outside the cave that is called Pulpet Rock where ministers would stand so they could preach to their congregations in the cave. In fact, the sound of a choir singing has been picked up on digital recorders during ghost investigations in the cave. Some believe she could be leftover from these early church-goers. Others conclude she may have been someone who fell off one of the high cliff walls.

The sound of drums have echoed through the cave, ghostly remnants of Ash Cave's past.

The sound of Native Indian drums echo off the walls of the recess cave long after visitors have left the cave.

There are several Native Indian burials within the recess cave. However, the cave has been used for centuries by Native Indians as a place to rest for the night. There was even a family of early white settlers that lived there for a short time.

Horsehead Grotto, the Thieves' Cave. Along the lower trail.

Conkle's Hollow State Nature Preserve

24132 Big Pine Road
Rockbridge, Ohio 43149
39.453492, -82.572727

Conkle's Hollow *is known to hikers for its sheer cliffs and unique hollows. There is an upper and lower trail. The lower trail is accessible to wheelchairs. The upper has sheer cliff faces.*

On the lower trail, there is a cave that was once called "Thieves Cave." Native Indians living in the area would rob settlers traveling through the area and hide their loot in the caves and hollows. Several of the thieves were caught, but not before they could hide their treasure in Conkle's Hollow. They were hung in the hollow and to this day, it is said you can see their shadows roaming up and down the trails and hear their faraway chatter above on the cliffs.

Hope Furnace (left) would have looked much like the restored Buckeye Furnace in Jackson, Ohio (below) when in operation.

Lake Hope State Park—Hope Iron Furnace

OH-278

McArthur, Ohio 45651

39.331976, -82.340552

Lake Hope State Park: Lake Hope State Park was once the home of the town of Hope Furnace. The stack from the iron furnace and an old cemetery are pretty much all remaining to remind us that a rather large company town existed there once. It is hard to believe that a fully-functioning iron furnace, general office, school, a post office, cemetery, workers' homes and saloons once dotted the landscape. But small remnants, like old wells and foundations, can be found just across Route 278 from the furnace by those with a keen eye.

Lake Hope has at least one legendary ghost. In all honesty, it is surprising there aren't more unrested spirits making themselves known where the town of Hope Furnace once stood. Furnace towns were notorious for harboring a rough crowd. Write-ups in old newspapers speak of fights at the saloons, unlucky souls hit by trains and . . . murders.

Murder Will Out. *Our readers will perhaps remember of the destruction by fire of a cabin, belonging to Hope Furnace Co., near Zaleski, some five years since, and that its two occupants, young men named Scott, were, it was reported and believed, burned to death in it. Later information leads to the conclusion that they were murdered. The developments are reported thus: John Slavens, who was working at Hope Furnace at the time of the fire went from there to Tennessee, where, lately, he murdered his nephew, for which he was tried, found guilty, and sentenced to the Penitentiary for a long term of years. Before, however, he was forwarded to the Penitentiary in accordance with his sentence, either he or his wife confessed to the murder of the two Scott boys and that he had fired the cabin to hide the deed, which was done for money. .* ***.The Vinton record., July 25, 1872. Murder Will Out***

Could the murders of the Scott boys be the explanation of the ghostly figure (left) showing up in this photo taken at the town of Hope Furnace? Just to the right of the apparition, a dark form appears to be watching...

But Lake Hope does have a ghost whose story has been passed down for over a hundred years. Most people have heard the story of the horrid fate of one of the Hope Furnace guards in the 1800s. His job was to walk the ledge of the iron furnace to keep people out and he fell to a fiery death inside. His ghost now walks above it with a lantern and the light can be seen bobbing up and down on the hillside.

But what a lot don't know is that for many years after his death, people claimed to not only see the lantern, but hear the ghost up there, his boots scratching and crunching in the dirt and along the stones.

When the general store was open near the base of the furnace, there would be knocks on the door at the same time of evening he was killed. When those inside answered the door, no one was there.

Moonville Tunnel.

Moonville Tunnel (Moonvilletunnel.com)

27331 State Route 278

McArthur, OH 45651

39.306443,-82.321286

Moonville was scarcely known as little more than just one tiny coal mining boom town among hundreds just like it in Southeastern Ohio. It came into existence with the Marietta and Cincinnati Railroad whose tracks crossed Vinton County right around 1856. During its prime in the mid-1800s, there was never more than a hundred people living in the tiny community and within a couple miles radius of its limits. The road leading to it, even then, was a rugged twisting and turning path just large enough for outlying farm wagons to make it to Samuel Coe's mill on the east side of Raccoon Creek or the Ferguson's farm on the west side where a tunnel would be built through a long section of Appalachian hillside.

The town itself had a saloon, depot, schoolhouse, strip of homes, and a cemetery. A tunnel was built through a hillside on the Henry Ferguson property, the infamous Moonville Tunnel. The town remained a little less than a hundred years until the last family left, leaving it nothing more than a ghost town among many in the declining economy of the 1940s.

The tunnel and the ghost town of Moonville is 20 miles from Old Man's Cave. Even if you can't see more of the town than a few old foundation stones and a well, it is well worth the drive to see the tunnel . . . and perhaps, a ghost or two. The spirit of an engineer, a brakeman, a woman hit by a train and a bully haunt the tunnel where more than 26 people have lost their lives over the last 160 years.

So who are these ghosts who haunt Moonville?

The Engineer: On a cold November night in 1880, Engineer Frank Lawhead was driving a train along the dark passage from Cincinnati to Marietta. He would have no more time than to blink at the tiny light bearing down on him before his life was stripped away.

The dispatcher failed to notify Engineer Lawhead that there was a second train coming toward them on the tracks. The train that Engineer Lawhead was driving along the Marietta and Cincinnati route through the tiny town of Moonville would take a headlong trip straight into another train coming along the same tracks. Engineer Lawhead died instantly.

> *Frank Lawhead, Engineer Killed in Train Wreck Near Kings station in this county on Thursday last, Engineer Lawhead and Charles Krick, fireman, both of Chillicothe, were instantly killed by collision of freight trains, which, we are told, was the result of a mistake of train dispatcher. The trains were totally wrecked.* ***Athens Messenger, Thursday, Nov 11, 1880.***

But he hasn't left those tracks in over 130 years. People have taken pictures of a man with a top hat at the far end of the tunnel. The sound of a train can be heard on some nights even though the tracks are long gone.

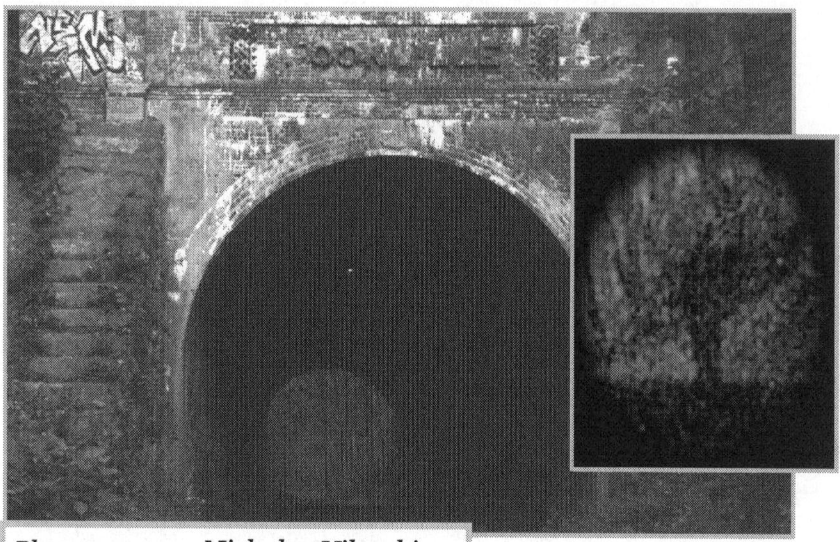

Photo courtesy: Nicholas Viltrakis.

About the Photo: A group of friends of mine (and I) were camping near lake hope 9/15/7 - 9/16/7 and we wanted to go on the haunted tour. It took us about two hours to find the train tunnel because we aren't the brightest or most organized, anyway. I am a professional photographer and I shot the whole weekend for fun. When we finally got to the easily found tunnel, I ran ahead to get a couple of shots of the spooky tunnel without people. I clicked off about 10 and then my group started filtering past me yelling through the tunnel. We ran all through the place and had a great time, I climbed it and posed on top and all. Nothing even remotely spooky or ghostly, nothing. Then when I was looking through the photos Sunday I was looking at them large and I noticed in this picture that there was the REAL figure of a person! We ran all through that tunnel and there was no one else there unless they were hiding in the woods until we left. Could be a shadow or tree or something, we really weren't checking around, we were mostly trying to scare each other and take pictures.
I did lighten the lower corner of the end of the tunnel after I saw the figure so you could see it better, and I have attached an enhanced version of the figure. **Nicholas Viltrakis**

The trail to Moonville is rugged. There is a small gravel area before the Moonville bridge where you can park. You will see a dirt path that you can follow at the pull-off. GPS: 39.31012,-82.324291

The Brakeman: The brakeman was usually a younger man between the ages of 16 and 25. He had a dangerous job assisting with braking the cars of the train. Many times, he had to ride atop more than one car to apply the brakes to the moving train, especially on the twists and turns, uphills and downhills of southeastern Ohio. His tasks also included lining up switches and signaling train operators.

There are at least four brakemen killed on the railway near Moonville Tunnel: An unknown brakeman in 1859 who fell from the cars due to "too free use of liquor." In 1873, a 21-year old brakeman by the name of McDevitt was caught between two colliding platforms and had both legs and one arm horribly mangled. He would later die. In 1876 Michael Molboro was killed and eight years later, his brother was killed on the same track.

Countless witnesses report they have seen a man carrying a lantern trudging along the tracks and through the tunnel, only to disappear just as he eases into a dark spot within the darkness. Some have even taken pictures at the tunnel when no one is around, only to find later the image of a man standing at the far end with what appears to be only one leg.

Moonville Bully: Baldy Keeton was from Moonville right around 1886. He was notorious for being a bully, picking on anyone smaller than his own size. His ghost story has been told by locals for more than a hundred years. He was sixty-five when he died and it was under suspicious circumstances—after returning from a court appearance in Zaleski, his body was found mangled on the tracks. Most believed he was dead before the train hit him. It is said his ghost has been seen above the tunnel, standing still and solitary. He has been known to throw rocks and pebbles at those walking beneath.

The ghost of Lavender Lady has been seen and . . . smelled at the far end of the tunnel.

Lavender Lady: The ghost of a woman is said to walk along the far side of the tracks, followed by the scent of lavender. Some describe her as an elderly woman, slightly bent and thin. She ambles across the gritty gravel where the tracks once stood before she vanishes from site. Her apparition is followed by a faint whiff of lavender perfume.

At least three women were killed on the tracks near Moonville. An unknown woman in 1873, in 1905 Mary Shea, of Moonville, aged 80 was struck by a train while trying to cross the trestle. And 76 year-old Deborah Allen was killed in 1890 by a funeral train carrying an engineer who had been killed in another train wreck.

Tools of the Trade—

Basic Ghost Tools:

Here you'll find the basic ghost equipment and a not-so-technical explanation of its use. But you can make up a pretty inexpensive ghost hunting kit, if you're on a budget, of simply an infrared camera and a digital recorder. These are the two simple tools that you can use on either a night or day ghost hunt or one at the spur of the moment. In fact, we've even seen some awesome images come from regular cell phones!

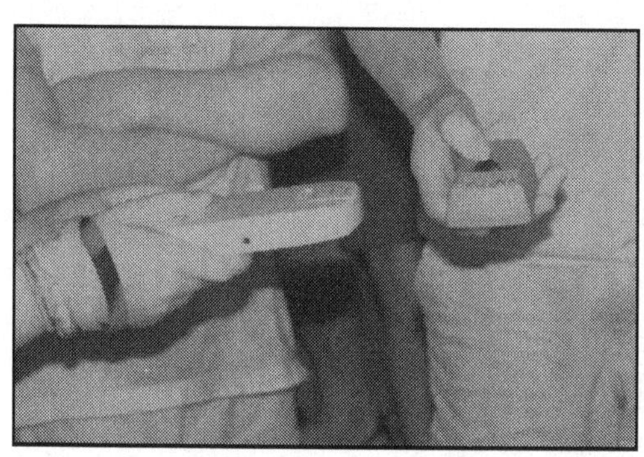

EMF Detector:
An EMF meter is a scientific instrument measuring fluctuations in electromagnetic fields –invisible lines of force produced by voltage and current. These fields are around us all the time in such electronics as computers, lights, televisions, electric lines and hair dryers. It is a common theory that ghosts contain some sort of electrical residue and/or they may be able to disrupt a field of energy. Such, the same kind of spikes showing a high electrical current caused by placing an EMF meter next to an electrical outlet could also be used to detect the presence of a spirit.

EMF detectors, in everyday use, are utilized for tracking and identifying high levels of electronic radiation that could quite possibly be hazardous. So if you get a spike on the EMF, it doesn't necessarily mean there is ghostly activity. Check for nearby outlets or sources of electricity. Cell phones, wall outlets and lights can cause a huge spike in the EMF detector. *Things to look for: Detector that makes a distinct sound to alert you of activity.*

Digital Recorder: Digital voice recorders are used to pick up audio that might not be heard with the human ear, or to validate audio heard during a session. Be careful in choosing a recorder. Although they are one of the least expensive tools a ghost hunter can buy, you want to make sure that it has a way to transfer files from the recorder to a computer for analysis. A recorder with a pop-out USB makes it easy to plug your recorder right into a computer and transfer files for reviewing. *Things to look for: USB Connection. Long Battery Life. Long recording time.*

Digital Cameras and Video Recorders: Digital cameras and video recorders allow the user to see things that are not viewable by the naked eye. Full spectrum cameras have no filtering. They can see the upper Near Ultraviolet, entire Visible spectrum, and Near Infrared spectrum. An infrared camera allows users to see into a different light spectrum. *Things to look for: This is one you will definitely want to check online reviews of the camera and see actual images.*

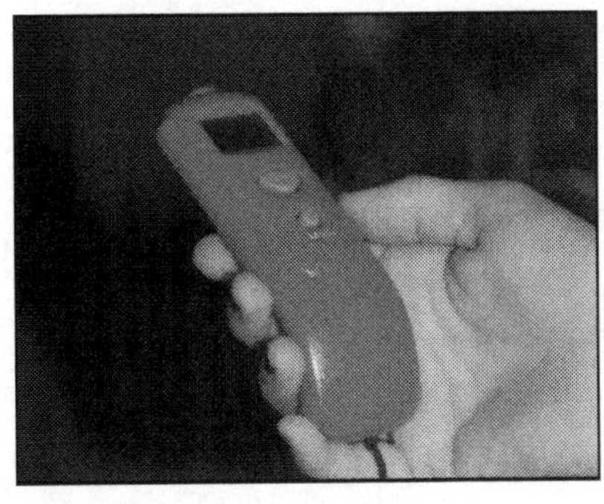

Thermometers: Digital thermometers allow ghost hunters to see sharp changes in temperatures. These dips and fluctuations are believed to be signs of paranormal activity. *Things to look for: Screen that lights up.*

Motion Sensors (infrared or ultrasound): Motion sensors can detect unusual movement in a region that may or may not be seen by the naked eye. *Things to look for: Long battery life.*

Spirit Box: A spirit box is a modified digital radio that sweeps through multiple audio channels, either on AM or FM bands. A mix of white noise (a staticy sound) and fragments of chatter like disk jockey voices and music can be heard by the user. It is believed spirits can either manipulate words passing through or that the radio waves simply help the ghost to communicate. Listen carefully for clear words and phrases above the jumble of radio sounds. *Things to look for: Make sure you buy the most up-to-date product. Purchase a speaker or earphones separately.*

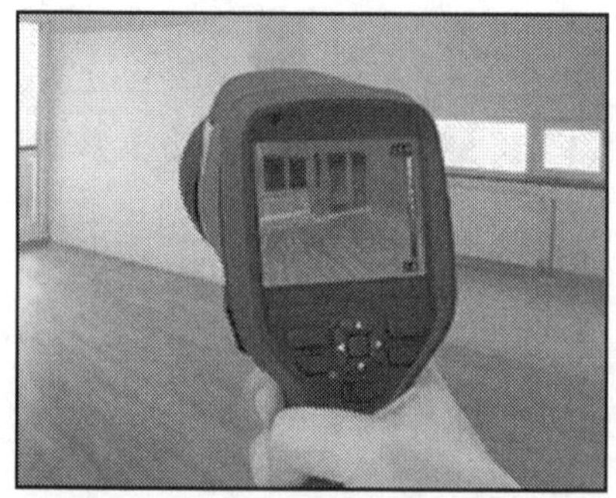

Thermal Imaging Infrared Camera: Thermal Imagers work by detecting levels of infrared energy radiating from different objects. They show a map of hot and cool surface temperatures. Different colors are used to distinguish differences in heat signatures in those objects so users can visualize temperature changes in the environment. *Things to look for: Imager with the ability to record. Large screen size.*

Ovilus: The theory behind the device is that spirits can manipulate the environment so that the ovilus comes up with an appropriate response, converting environmental readings into real words. It has a preset database of words from which to choose. One thing to watch for—many times, the ovilus seems to just thrust out random words that those listening can manipulate to fit the situation. You have to make sure that you aren't just taking the words through power of suggestion and working a story around your questions. *Things to look for: Reviews*

Trail Camera with Night Vision: Motion-sensor digital camera/video camera that can be tethered to a tree or set on about any stationary object like a chair or table. These are great to set out to cover more area during a ghost investigation, to cover areas where humans might discourage interaction, or to appraise areas before an investigation. The camera is triggered by any movement and works great to find out if perhaps that bumping in the attic are flying squirrels banging off the ceiling instead of dead Aunt Ada coming back to haunt her next of kin. *Things to look for: Long battery life. Infrared ability.*

Other equipment/tools: Flashlight: Some believe you can communicate with a spirit by setting a flashlight on a table and unscrewing it so the slightest touch will turn it on, then asking the spirit to turn the light on or off in response to specific questions (lights up twice for "yes", and once for "no"). You may also need this tool to read the meters if they do not have a screen that lights up. **Audacity:** Audio editing application for your computer.

Citations—

Citations:

Adams County:

Cherry Fork Cemetery

-Cleveland Plain Dealer, Historical Archives August 12, 1896 A Grave Yawns.
-The News-Herald. Hillsboro, Oh. January 18, 1894. Couldn't Get His Breath
-News-Herald. Hillsboro, Oh. Thursday December 27, 1893 Parker Confesses
-The Evening World. New York, NY. January 12, 1894, BROOKLYN LAST EDITION, HANGED BY BEST CITIZENS. Boy Murderer Victim of Mob Law in Ohio
-The News-Herald. Hillsboro, Oh. December 28, 1893, Page 5. An Awful Double Crime
-The Evening Bulletin. Maysville, KY. December 27, 1893.
-The Evening Bulletin. Maysville, KY. December 23, 1893. Lynching Liable
-The Ohio Democrat. Logan, Ohio. December 30 1993. Parker Confesses
-Alexandria Gazette. Alexandria, Virginia. December 23, 1893. Telegraphic Brevities
-A History of Adams County, Ohio: From Its Earliest Settlement to the Present Time, Including Character Sketches of the Prominent Persons Identified with the First Century of the Country's Growth ... By Nelson Wiley Evans, Emmons B. Stivers Nelson Wiley Evans, Emmons B. Stivers .1900 - Adams Co(Ohio)
-ancestry.com. Parker Family Tree.
-Findagrave.com—Luther Pitt Rhine. http://www.findagrave.com/cgi-bin/fg.cgi?page=gr&GSln=rhine&GSiman=1&GScid=189064&GRid=44269387&
- Roscoe Parker Grave: http://www.ohiogenealogyexpress.com/adams/adamsco_hist_pt2_chptxiii_waynentwp.htm

Ashland County:

Katotawa Creek

-uglybridges.com/1395428.
-http://www.times-gazette.com/local%20news/2008/10/25/historic-ashland-area-s-ghoulish-past-still-haunts-residents-plenty-of-spooky-reasons-to-keep-your-lights-on-this-halloween. Historic Ashland/Area's ghoulish past still haunts residents/Plenty of spooky reasons to keep your lights on this Halloween
Published: October 25, 2008 . Ashland Times Gazette.
-History of Ashland County, Ohio, Volume 1, Baughman, Abraham J. S.J. Clarke Publishing Company. 1909.

Haunted Tunnel

-http://seekinglostsouls.com/category/ohiohauntings/page/4/
-https://www.youtube.com/watch?v=AFVIpgpIkk4, Ashland Tunnel, Twp rd 1536. Brd Pritt. Nov 15, 2009

Landolls Mohican Castle

-Landoll, Jimmy. Property Owner interview.
-http://www.findagrave.com/cgi-bin/fg.cgi?page=cr&CRid=2315225
-http://files.usgwarchives.net/oh/ashland/cemeteries/heyd.txt
-Colvin, Lee. Property Owner and Historian.
Permanent Resident. http://theresashauntedhistoryofthetri-state.blogspot.com/2012_02_01_archive.html

Athens:
Philadelphia Inquirer) October 14, 1889: Spooks and Spirits
Brown:
Cleveland Plain Dealer. (Cleveland, Oh) Historical Archives. February 9, 1895. Followed By Ghostly Hounds
Butler County:
Collinsville Cemetery
-Cincinnati Enquirer September 14, 1890. Page 10. A Headless Ghost Perched on a Sycamore Stump with Blood Streaming Down its Body.
-Milford Township Map 1888 -Milford Township Map 1875
Rossville
-The Journal News (Hamilton, Ohio). October 26, 1971 Page 64 Hamilton's Early Burial Grounds Hidden
-Blount, Jim. Journal-News (Hamilton, Ohio) May 11, 1994
-Hamilton City Ward 1 Map, 1875
- Cincinnati Enquirer (Cincinnati, Ohio) July 27, 1890. A Ten-Foot Ghost Seen in the Old Boudinot Cemetery
-Blount, Jim. Journal News. Oct. 23, 2002 -- Haunted house search turned fatal for student in 1962:
Hangman's Hollow
-Lindley, Fred. Darrtown.com. 7/17/2105. Image: Alice (Kramer) Miller
-Heiser, Alta Harvey. Hamilton Daily News Journal 08 17 1961. Butler County History. Hangman's Hollow Hangman's Hollow Received Its Name In July Of 1829 With The Death Of Martin Koble; Brother Of Deceased Received Estate After He Was Found Two Years Later
-Hamilton Daily Republican News. (Hamilton, Ohio) Wednesday, October 05, 1910. Legend of Hangman's Hollow
-Info collected by Samantha Harris, Public Services Associate, Smith Library of Regional History. The Lane Libraries. Oxford, OH 45056
-The Journal News from Hamilton, Ohio. August 16, 1975. Page 28
-Hamilton Daily Democrat April 26, 1892 Hangman's Hollow
-Hamilton Daily Democrat. September 05, 1892 Hangman's Hollow
-Hamilton Daily Democrat October 18, 1893 Hangman's Hollow
-Hamilton Daily News Journal October 15, 1950. Hangman's Hollow
Champaign County:
Evergreen Cemetery
-PIQUA DAILY CALL. Piqua, Oh. RUMOR HAS IT. September 15, 1973.
Lincoln Ghost Train
-Ghost-Hunting Groups Enjoy Renewed Popularity. Hannah, James. Associated Press.
Columbiana County:
-Little Beaver River valleys, Pennsylvania -- Ohio with illustrated check list of flowers and essays. By members of Robin Hood Club and Ira F. Mansfield : At head of title: Historical collections : Historical collections, Little Beaver River valleys : Pennsylvania history. 1914.
-The Evening Review. East Liverpool, Ohio. March 1, 1975.
-Gard, Max and Vodrey, William Jr. The Sandy & Beaver Canal.
Gretchen's Lock and Esther Hale
-Little Beaver River valleys, Pennsylvania -- Ohio with illustrated check list of flowers and essays. By members of Robin Hood Club and Ira F. Mansfield Historical collections, Little Beaver River valleys Pa. 1914.
-The Evening Review. East Liverpool, Ohio. March 1, 1975.
-Gard, Max and Vodrey, William Jr. The Sandy & Beaver Canal.

Columbiana County (cont'd)
Pretty Boy Floyd:
-Charles "Pretty Boy" Floyd. (2015). The Biography.com website. Retrieved 04:01, May 14, 2015, from http://www.biography.com/people/charles-pretty-boy-floyd-9542085.
-Beaver Creek State Park. http://www.graveaddiction.com/beavercr.html
Cuyahoga County:
-Giometti, Paul F. http://www.paintedhills.org/STEUBEN/WaylandTrainWreck.html. Painted Hills Genealogy Society The Wreck of the Lackawanna Limited at Wayland, NY on August 30, 1943
-THE NEW YORK TIMES, New York. AUGUST 31, 1943. 23 DIE IN COLLISION ON LACKWANNA; LIMITED DERAILED
-http://www.newsnet5.com/news/local-news/my-ohio/passenger-train-car-from-1943-crash-haunts-midwest-railway-preservation-society-in-cleveland. Leon Bibb, newsnet5.com . September 6, 2013.
-The Pittsburgh Press - Aug 31, 1943. Volunteer Women-Workers Killed.
Fairfield County:
-http://www.nitemarecafe.com/2013/09/the-clarksburg-ghost.html
-Turner, Herbert M. . Fairfield County Remembered: The Early Years. Ohio University Special Publications, 1999. The Lonely Grave On Allen's Knob. The Clarksburg Ghost.
Shimp's Hill
-FAIRFIELD COUNTY CHAPTER of the OHIO GENEALOGICAL SOCIETY. http://www.fairfieldgenealogy.org/research/resea.html
-1849 Plat Map—Fairfield County, Richland Township.
-Newark Advocate. Remember when-Shimp's Hill. Apr. 23, 2012. http://www.newarkadvocate.com/article/BD/20120423/NEWS01/204230307
-Shimp, Nicholas. http://www.genealogy.com/
-Eagle Gazette, Lancaster Ohio. 1950. The Legend Of Shimp's Hill
Franklin:
Schiller Park
-Repository. Canton, OH.14 November 1894. Suicided in Park.
-Der Deutsche Correspondent., November 19, 1894, Translator: Margit Chevalier.
-Cincinnati Enquirer December 5, 1894 page 4. Has No Head
Old Governor's Mansion
-The Columbus Foundation. http://columbusfoundation.org/about/history/
-Ohio Governor's Mansion/Lindenburg House Haunted Houses . 10/17/2013. http://www.hauntedhouses.com/states/oh/ohio_mansion.htm
-Adams, Janet. Columbus Business First. American City Business Journals. Columbus' haunted houses. Mar 6, 2014. Old Governor's Mansion
http://www.bizjournals.com/columbus/
Greene:
-Springfield Globe-Republic., August 22, 1885
-Cleveland Plain Dealer, Historical Archives. March 20, 1886
-The Jackson Standard. (Jackson C.H., Ohio), August 27, 1885

Greene County (cont'd)
-Globe Republic August 22, 1885 The Deadly Shot Gun. Quarrel Between Two Greene County Farmers
-Springfield Globe-Republic., January 09, 1886. The Penitentiary for Life
-Springfield Globe-Republic., March 16, 1886. Scared at a Ghost
-Xenia Daily Gazette from Xenia, Ohio. November 28, 1906. Page 8. THANKSGIVING PARDON OF GOVERNOR HARRIS Foils on a Greene County Man—Life Prisoner, Old and Gray, Returns Home After Twenty Years Penal Service.
Hamilton County:
Hand Alley
-Cincinnati Enquirer April 1, 1889 Page 8. A REAL GHOST.
Congress Green
-The Saint Paul Globe., November 20, 1904. Famous Men's Sons Who Have Made Good.
-Van Beck, Todd W. THE HARRISON HORROR, GRAVE ROBBING AND THE INVENTION OF THE BURIAL VAULT
-The Cincinnati daily Star., June 06, 1878, Third Edition. Harrison Horror
-The Findlay Jeffersonian., June 07, 1878. The Grave Robbed
Hardin:
Hog Creek Swamp:
-The Ada Herald 1978-10-25- Page 11 Dola Marsh ghost
Henry:
Buckland Lock/Lock 44
-Akron Daily Democrat. July 21, 1902, Page 5. A Weird Tale of the Canal Locks Near Napoleon
Highland:
Dunn Chapel
-The News-Herald., September 06, 1888. What Is It? What An Honest Farmer Saw at Midnight in a Country Graveyard.
Fallsville
-Penn Township, Careytown, Dodsonville, Samantha, Russel, Boston, Fairview: Highland County 1916H
-Highland County Map: 1887
-Rootsweb.com
-Findagrave.com
-Buckeye Legends: Folktales and lore from Ohio By Michael Jay Katz
Leesburg
-The Highland Weekly News., April 15, 1885.
Hocking County:
Scotts Creek
-The Ohio Democrat., August 20, 1887. Deadly Gulf
-The Hocking sentinel., August 18, 1887, Image 3
-The Hocking sentinel., March 03, 1887
Old Man's Cave
-The Hocking Sentinel. June 22, 1905. The Wonderland of Hocking Dead Man's Cave
-Logan Hocking Sentinel July 21, 1853

Hocking County: (cont'd)

Old Man's Cave

-The Democrat-sentinel., August 12, 1909
-The Democrat-sentinel., August 15, 1907
-The Democrat-sentinel., February 25, 1909
-The Democrat-sentinel., March 28, 1907 Interesting Story of Old Man's Cave
-The Hocking sentinel., June 22, 1905, Image 4 old man hid money

Jackson County:

Berlin Crossroads

-Cincinnati Enquirer Author SPECIAL DISPATCH TO THE ENQUIRER Sep 12, 1894 page 1
-Jackson County Engineers Office. Historical land owners Berlin Crossroads.

Fairmount Cemetery

-The Jackson standard., October 06, 1881. A Spook

Jefferson County:

Nancy Weir

Belmont chronicle., June 10, 1886 death
-Cleveland Plain Dealer. Historical Archives. 1888-03-10
-Cleveland Plain Dealer. Historical Archives. March 10, 1888 A

Drummers Yarn

-Belmont chronicle., June 10, 1886, Image 3
-The Stark County Democrat., June 10, 1886, Image 1
-The Cadiz sentinel., June 19, 1867, Image 3 The Semi Weekly Age 1886_04_19_0002 Coshocton

Knox County:

-Cincinnati Enquirer, Special Dispatch to the Enquirer. November 21, 1897 Page 17. Strange Apparition of a Man That Guards the Spring at —
Camp Sychar Holiness Camp: www.campsychar.org/

Licking County:

-Researchers: Glosser, Eric. Christy, Carla. Duke, Michelle. http://www.parajail.com/

Lorain County:

Cottesbrooke Curve Wreck

-Zimmerman, S. Wayne County Historical Society & Museum. ORIGINS OF A SOUTHWESTERN "GREEN LINE" GHOST STORYwaynehistoricalohio.org/2013/10/19/origins-of-a-southwestern-green-line-ghost-story/
-The Elyria Chronicle, Elyria, Ohio Monday July 20, 1903. Electric Car Telescoped. Fatal Collision at the Black River Bridge in Carlisle.
—Wooster Weekly Republican. January 27, 1904. Pg 5. Ghost Story
-Wayne County Public Library: www.wcpl.info

Lucas County:

-Weber, Lauren. Toledo Blade. http://www.toledoblade.com/frontpage/2007/06/17/Beneath-the-beams-abutments-and-concrete-Toledo-s-Maumee-crossings-have-a-story-to-tell.html
-Cincinnati Enquirer Dec 28, 1884. A Ghost on the Bridge

Mahoning County:
Hazelton and Struthers Ghost
Cincinnati Enquirer SPECIAL DISPATCH TO THE ENQUIRER Oct 14, 1891 page 9
Medina County:
-Totts, Judy A. Remembering Medina County. Tales from Ohio's Western Reserve. The History Press, 2009. Sharon Township: The Ghost of Lottie Bader.
-Sharon Township
Ottawa County:
-Andra-Hogeland, Brandy. Toledo Haunted Places Examiner. Soldiers may still reside on the Johnsons Island Cemetery.http://www.examiner.com/article/soldiers-may-still-reside-on-the-johnsons-island-cemetery
-Johnson's Island Preservation Society. www.johnsonsisland.org
-Donmoyer, Ryan J. New York Times. Archipelago of Legends and Play. August 13, 2000 pg. TR10
Preble County:
-Howe, Henry. Historical Collections of Ohio: In Three Volumes ; an Encyclopedia of the State ... : with Notes of a Tour Over it in 1886 ... Contrasting the Ohio of 1846 with 1886-90, Volume 3 . Henry Howe and Sons, 1891.
-Historic Maps—Preble County, Somers 1871, Publisher: Co Titus.
-The Democratic Banner., June 03, 1913. (Mt Vernon, Ohio). Farmhand Arrested.
-The Marion Daily Star (Marion, Ohio). October 22, 1913.
-Hamilton Telegraph. (Hamilton, Ohio). October 23, 1913. Davis on Trial for Murder of Franklin Bourne.
-Hamilton Evening Journal. (Hamilton, Ohio). October 14, 1913
-Preble County Convention and Visitors Bureau. www.preblecountypassport.com/ghost_hunting.html
-Beougher, Stephanie. Court News Now. HAPPENING NOW. Haunted Ohio Courthouses. October 28, 2013
-Preble County District Library. 450 S. Barron St; Eaton, OH 45320
-"Preble County: Celebrating Our Heritage One Township At A Time As Told By Those Who Lived It" Preble County, Ohio/Kee Printing, Incorporated, 2008.
Ross County:
-Darby, Erasmus Foster. The Ghost of Enos Kay. Chillicothe, Ohio : published privately by Dave Webb, 1953. Series: Ohio folklore series, no. 8.
-Ross County Historical Society. McKell Library, Chillicothe, Ohio.
Scioto County:
-Harry Knighton, "Shawnee Forest," undated typescript, Digital History Lab Collection, Clark Memorial Library, Shawnee State University, Portsmouth, Ohio.
-SPECIAL DISPATCH TO THE ENQUIRER. Cincinnati Enquirer July 17, 1888. WOMAN AND CHILD.
-Andrew Lee Feight, Ph.D., "The Drummer's Ghost in Dead Man Hollow ,"Scioto Historical, accessed July 1, 2015, http://sciotohistorical.org/items/show/38.
-Portsmouth Times May 31, 1948 . Grave In the 'Wilds' Of Scioto Co Holds Secret

Summit County:

Breitenstine Park

-Perkins, Simon. Centennial history of Summit County, Ohio and representative citizens. Biographical Publishing Company. 1908
-Akron daily Democrat., August 08, 1902, Page 2. Norton Ghost
-The Stark County Democrat., August 12, 1902, WEEKLY EDITION, Page 8 Weird Visitors.
-Summit County Historical Maps. 1891 and 1901. Norton Township.

Akron County:

-Albrecht, John Jr. Cleveland Haunted Places Examiner. Hunting the haunted: Akron's Lock 3. January 16, 2013
-Past Pursuits A Newsletter of the Special Collections Division of the Akron-Summit County Public Library. Autumn 2007. An Akron Haunting. sc.akronlibrary.org/files/2011/03/pursuits63.pdf

Bailey Bridge

-http://cuyahogafallshistory.com/2013/03/murder-by-the-doodlebug/
-Holland, Jeri. Historian. Cuyahoga Falls Historical Society 2015. based off a written interview with Gilbert Roberts, local history and court transcripts. Cuyahoga Falls Historical Society 2015 http://cuyahogafallshistory.com/2014/10/the-headless-ghost-on-bailey-road/
-The Ohio star., Ravenna, Ohio. April 20, 1853 Supposed Murder of a Stranger-Evidences of Foul Play
-Wheeling daily intelligencer., April 26, 1853. Horrid Murder.
-True American., June 13, 1855 Steubenville, Ohio Execution of Parks
-The Ohio star., January 18, 1854. Parks Sentenced
-The Belmont Chronicle, and Farmers, Mechanics and Manufacturers advocate., January 27, 1854. Conviction and Sentence of Parks.
-The Bench and Bar of Cleveland. Page 96
-The Last Days of Cleveland: And More True Tales of Crime and Disaster from By John Stark Bellamy

Everett Road Covered Bridge

-www.nps.gov/.../**everett**-road-**covered-bridge**
-The Stark County Democrat, Canton, Ohio. February 15, 1877.

Doodlebug Disaster

--Albrecht, John Jr. Cleveland Haunted Places Examiner. Hunting the haunted: Hunting the haunted: Cuyahoga Falls' Doodlebug Disaster. August 12, 2012.

Glen Bridge

-http://mredmountainline.blogspot.com/

Mary Campbell Cave

-http://www.ohiohistorycentral.org/w/Mary_Campbell_Cave?rec=3114
-Butler, Margaret Manor. *A Pictorial History of the Western Reserve: 1796-1860*. Cleveland, OH: The Early Settlers Association of the Western Reserve and The Western Reserve Historical Society, 1963.

Indian Signal Tree

-Summit Metro Parks. http://www.summitmetroparks.org/ParksAndTrails/CascadeValleySouth.aspx

Summit County: (cont'd)
The Town of Botzum
-Lane, Samuel Alanson. Fifty Years and Over of Akron and Summit County [O.] The Killing of John Tedrow by Thomas Brook
-Breckenridge, Mary Beth. Akron Beacon Journal. Nine haunted sites you can visit in Akron area. Waterways Council, Inc. http://cqrcengage.com/wci/app/document/4682258;jsessionid=jMcLytZokKG6opww6-NNdQon.undefined
-The Wheeling daily intelligencer., October 30, 1882. Murder in Akron
-The Stark County Democrat, November 2, 1882 1 Murder at a Ball.
-The Democratic press., Ravenna, Ohio. November 02, 1882
-The Stark County Democrat, November 2, 1882. Murder at a Ball.
-ProQuest Historical Newspapers: The Cincinnati Enquirer CLEVELAND.: Fatal Shooting Affray at Botzum. Disastrous Wreck on the ... SPECIAL DISPATCH TO THE ENQUIRER Cincinnati Enquirer (1872-1922); Oct 29, 1882;
Trumbull County:
-Summit County Beacon (Akron, OH) February 4, 1885: p. 5 Ghosts Along the Border
-Elyria Republican (Elyria, Ohio) January 29, 1885. A Blood Curdling Story
-Davis, Andrew Jackson. BOSTON: COLBT & BICH, FUBLISHEBS, 1885. Harvard University. Beyond the Valley: A Sequel to "The Magic Staff": an Autobiography of Andrew Jackson Davis.
-Trumbull County (Ohio) Records Center and Archive Dept. Trumbull County Ohio. Historical Maps for Vernon Township—1830, 1840, 1850, 1859, 1870, 1874.
Vinton:
-Athens Sunday Messenger March 11, 1923
-Republican Enquirer. (McArthur, Ohio) March 29, 1920. Vinton County. 114 Years Ago in Vinton County History, By Our Route 2 Correspondent.
Washington County:
-Year: *1870*; Census Place: *Marietta Ward 2, Washington, Ohio*; Roll: *M593_1279*; Page: *332B*; Image: *159*; Family History Library Film: *552778*
-Catalog: 1946- Marietta College Bulletin, Marietta College. Publ 1879
-Racer, Theresa. The Buckley House's
Wyandot County:
Crawford Monument
-Marvin, Ron.. Wyandot County Historical Society.
-Wyandot County Map 1879 Harrison and Hare .1879 . Clark Township. Shows original monument area.
-Baughman, Abraham J. Past and Present of Wyandot County, Ohio: A Record of Settlement, Organization, Progress and Achievement. 1913
Images: rudall30, ljupco, Jeffrey Banke , Vladimir Nikulin, Raisa Yana Zastols, Kanareva, Ysbrand Cosijn, Mikhail Pogosov , Rommel Canlas , Shannon Fagan, Stokkete,Jozef Polc, Vadim Guzhva, Alan Poulson, Suljo, Elnur Amikishiyev. Library of Congress Prints and Photographs Division Washington, D.C. 20540—nclc 0067, *LC-USF34-000589-ZB, Sydney Quackenbush*

Made in the USA
Charleston, SC
24 June 2016